Also by Vicki Stevenson:

The Family of Choice series
*Family Values*
*Family Affairs*
*Family Ties*

Other Titles
*Certain Personal Matters*
*Callie's Dilemma*

# April's Fool

## Vicki Stevenson

*Yellow Rose*
*by Regal Crest*

Texas

ISBN 978-1-61929-192-8


First Printing 2014

9 8 7 6 5 4 3 2 1


Cover design by AcornGraphics


Published by:

Regal Crest Enterprises, LLC
229 Sheridan Loop
Belton, Texas 76513


Find us on the World Wide Web at
http://www.regalcrest.biz


Published in the United States of America

# Acknowledgments

For long hours of beta reading and constructive criticism, I thank Marlene Kenyon, Hal McBride, Nancy Lantier, Mavis Chalmers and Dianne Kleppinger.

Editor Heather Flournoy worked extensively on the manuscript and taught me a tremendous amount. Her expertise in linguistics was especially helpful. Her infinite patience with my "point of view" problems is much appreciated. Thanks, Heather.

Finally, there is the one whose love and support keep me going through thick and thin. That is Sara Lynde, my partner, my best friend, the love of my life, and now my lawfully wedded wife. Thank you, my love.

# Dedication

For Sara: after a twenty-one year engagement, the honeymoon begins.

# Chapter One
## *Arizona Territory, 1886*

THE FINAL FIVE hours of my trip were the worst by far. A few miles outside of Phoenix, the road became narrow, rough and deeply rutted. The stagecoach bounced about so violently that I was afraid it might fly into a million pieces at any moment. I was afraid the horses might stumble and cause a horrible accident, despite the driver's repeated assurances that they were used to the pace and the condition of the trail. I was afraid we might be attacked by hostile natives, although that was supposedly a rare occurrence, thanks to the U. S. Army.

Even if I survived the trip, I had begun to doubt my own judgment. The more I thought about my carefully laid plan, the more foolish it seemed. The possibility that a young woman who had lived her entire life in the civilized city of St. Louis could succeed at what I was planning seemed suddenly quite unlikely indeed. Perhaps I deserved whatever fate awaited me in the godforsaken desert mining outpost of Weaver's Flat.

As we bounced along, mile after dreadful mile, I had a fanciful thought that perhaps I was already dead and didn't realize it. Perhaps I had been killed when the horses made a fatal misstep and I had been thrown from the coach. Perhaps I had been scalped by a band of marauding Apache Indians. Perhaps I was riding in a stagecoach from hell, where I would continue for eternity. The pieces seemed to fit. It was too hot, too dry, too dusty and just plain too miserable. I couldn't imagine a time and place more wretched than summer in the Arizona desert.

A sudden change caught my attention. The horses quickened their pace and I heard Amos, the driver, command them to slow down. I looked out the window and watched with a mixture of relief and trepidation as the town came into view.

Amos brought the horses to a stop at a wooden building whose sign proclaimed it to be the Weaver's Flat Post Office, Telegraph Station and Assay Office (Amanda Wells, Proprietor). I had never seen a woman who looked quite like the one who emerged carrying a large canvas bag marked "U.S. Mail." I had never seen a woman in trousers, and I was fascinated. She was tall and slender. She wore her auburn hair tied back with a piece of rawhide at the base of her neck. She wasn't pretty, exactly. She was...striking. That was it. She was striking, with her deeply tanned face and piercing gray eyes. She wore buckskin trousers, a faded green flannel shirt and black leather boots.

Amos jumped down from the coach, then opened the passenger

compartment door and helped me to the ground. He turned to the woman in buckskin. "Howdy, Mandy. Gimme a hand here?"

"Sure thing." Her voice was soft, yet firm and assured.

Mandy. So this was Amanda Wells, the woman Seth had told me about. Seth was certain that what he had heard firsthand from the two young brothers he'd met in St. Louis was true. Amanda Wells knew everything there was to know regarding what went on in Weaver's Flat, the nearby Superstition Mountains and the surrounding Apache Indian country. I intended to learn a great deal from her.

Amos unfastened the straps that secured the cargo to the back of the coach. Amanda hefted one of my bags and carried it to the wooden sidewalk, followed closely by Amos with my second bag and the mail sack from the Phoenix post office.

She stopped at the door and turned. "Um...where is this supposed to go, Amos?"

I took a deep breath and hoped my voice was steady. "Can you just put my things inside for now?" I asked.

"Sure, we can do that," she said with a smile.

As soon as my luggage hit the floor, Amos seemed eager to leave. Amanda helped him secure the outgoing mail sack and two small, very heavy wooden crates to the back of the coach.

"Will you be over at Emery's for awhile?" she asked him.

He shook his head. "I'm running behind. I'll only be at the livery stable as long as it takes to water and check the horses."

She looked outside, then back at him. "Okay. Mike Stander hasn't shown up yet with his weekly letter to his grandpa, so I suppose he'll just have to wait 'til next week to send it on its way."

"Sorry, Mandy, I'm behind already. Tell Mike I'm sorry I couldn't wait. If I don't leave soon, I won't make it back to Phoenix by nightfall."

Amos wished me well and said goodbye to us, then headed for the livery stable. I was left alone with Amanda Wells, and although I was not aware of it at the time, the greatest adventure of my life was about to begin.


FROM THE WINDOW of the post office, I watched the stagecoach as it rumbled up the street toward the local saloon. Presumably the livery stable was nearby. I turned around and surveyed the room.

The only chairs were behind the counter, in the rear part of the building that was obviously used for the business of assaying gold brought in by local prospectors. Amanda cocked her head and appeared to study me. I smiled at her and said nothing.

After several seconds she said, "Would you like some coffee? I was just about to make a fresh pot."

She went behind the counter and continued to the rear. I took it as an invitation and followed. I hoped that we could sit comfortably and that I could get better acquainted with the enigmatic Amanda Wells.

"I don't want to impose on your hospitality. My name is April Reynolds, and I would be pleased if you would permit me to make the coffee."

She was clearly taken aback. "*You* would make a pot of coffee?"

"Of course," I said. "Why wouldn't I?"

She seemed to relax, and the hint of a smile appeared on her face. "That was foolish of me. It's just that we don't often see ladies like you this far from Phoenix. The only women in town here are the ones who stay over at Emery's Saloon and they're—well, never mind. They're not like you."

She placed a few small mesquite branches into the stove and watched them as the fire took hold. "Most of the ranchers have wives, but they're also completely different from you."

"Amanda, I don't understand what you mean," I said as I took the coffeepot from the adjacent shelf and filled it with fresh water from a bucket on the rear counter. I was disconcerted. I had hoped to blend in easily with the local population.

"Call me Mandy, please. I'll tell you quite frankly that you're the most attractive woman ever to set foot in Weaver's Flat. It's not just your looks. It's your clothing, and everything about you. You don't look like anyone from Arizona."

I realized what she meant. My dark wool dress, the latest fashion in St. Louis, certainly wasn't appropriate for the hard life and work of a rancher's wife. Nor did I have the appearance of the "working girls" at Emery's Saloon. As I prepared the coffee, I sensed that the moment was rapidly approaching when I would have to explain my presence in the remote desert outpost.

Moments later I was relieved to hear the stagecoach pass outside. Apparently the horses had been watered and pronounced fit for the return trip to Phoenix. There would be no stagecoach out of Weaver's Flat for another week. I took two mugs from the shelf and filled them with coffee.

Mandy sipped cautiously, then grinned. "Perfect."

I said, "It's kind of you to let me wait here. I expected that Mr. Fletcher would be here to meet me when I arrived."

"Fletcher? You mean Norm Fletcher?" She frowned.

"Yes. The Fletchers want to send their sons to college in the East, so they hired me to prepare them for their entrance examinations. It was a difficult decision for me, this being such a remote area and all, but—"

"This isn't good." She turned away for a few seconds, then turned back. "The Fletchers died three months ago when their ranch burned down. Their sons survived, and they were sent to St. Louis to live with their aunt and uncle."

I looked at her intently. "Then I have nowhere to go. I have nowhere to stay. How can I even...how will I...?" I shook my head. "Oh,

Lord, I'll have to go back to Phoenix right away! Then I'll wire the placement agency and find out what they want to do about this."

She said, "I'm sorry. I'm afraid you're stranded here until the stagecoach comes back next week."

I bit my lower lip. "Then I'll just have to take a room and wait. You do have a boarding house in this town, don't you?"

"Um...well, not exactly," she murmured. "The only rooms are the ones over the saloon and they're just for...well, you can't stay there."

"Do you mean there's not anyplace where I can stay?"

She snapped her fingers. "You can stay at my place. There's plenty of room out there." She shrugged. "You might even enjoy it."

"I won't enjoy it, but I'm grateful for the offer," I said. I glanced at the two large suitcases that still lay where they had been dumped. "Can someone deliver my things to your...place?"

"Yes, and that 'someone' would be me," she said with a chuckle. "Now, here's what I have to do. Daisy, my horse, is over at the livery stable. I'll ride her home, hitch her up to my wagon, and come back here. Daisy can take us and your luggage back to my place as soon as I close up here for the day."

I said nothing, but nodded in agreement.

"You need to stay here in case anybody comes in," she continued. "You can handle the post office part — just play it by ear. Now, the assay office, that's a different matter. If anybody brings in gold for weighing and shipping, tell them I'll be back in an hour."

"Gold? I...I'm not sure I can —"

"Don't worry about that part. Everybody knows this is the day Amos picks up the weekly gold shipment. I don't think anybody will bring in more for the next few days. You'll be fine. I'll be back with Daisy and the wagon shortly."

"But I don't know anything about..." I watched Mandy jog away, presumably headed for the livery stable.

I turned back and began to explore the interior of the small building. It was a curious combination of post office, telegraph station, assay office and weekly stage stop. The woman who ran it all, improbably dressed in men's clothing and boots, maintained the operation in a state of optimal organization and functionality.

I BREATHED A sigh of relief when Mandy appeared about an hour later on a flatbed wagon pulled by a large chestnut mare. "Nobody came," I said when she entered. "And there was no noise from the telegraph machine either."

She laughed. "I'm glad to hear that. I can close up here in a couple of hours, and then we can go home. No special stops today."

"Special stops?" I wondered if this involved the information I sought.

"When the prospectors bring in gold, I weigh it and record the details, and at the end of the day I take it all over to the bank for safekeeping. Then on the morning of the stage pickup, like today, I bring it back here for Amos to take to Phoenix. So this afternoon I don't have any gold to take to the bank."

The rest of the afternoon passed quickly. A man came in to send a wire to San Francisco, and I got to observe Mandy's expertise with the mysterious telegraph machine. She gave me a pencil and paper to write out a message for my placement agency in St. Louis, but the matter was soon forgotten when a steady trickle of townspeople came in to pick up their mail.

As the sun began to fall behind the nearby mountains, she carried my suitcases outside to the wagon. She jumped up onto the front seat. She told me where to put my foot on the other side of the wagon, then pulled me up. I landed with an uncomfortable thud against the pistol she wore, and only then did the thought occur to me that a loaded gun was a necessity for Mandy's job.

ALTHOUGH THE SUN was nearly gone, the desert heat remained oppressive. Without a command, Daisy pulled the wagon around and set out for home at a slow pace. In less than fifteen minutes, a homestead came into view.

"Here we are," Mandy said cheerfully.

I was amazed. "It's lovely! I don't know why I imagined you'd live in an old rundown cabin. This is just... wonderful."

It was a large, well maintained adobe structure with a wooden porch. There were two windows in front and two on the north side. A small barn stood about fifty feet to the rear.

Mandy brought Daisy to a stop at the front door. She jumped off the wagon and reached up for me. After an awkward hesitation, I put my hands on her shoulders. She lifted me off the wagon and placed me gently on the ground.

"Let's get you and your things inside, then you can look around and get settled while I see to Daisy," she said.

The comfortably furnished house reflected the style and needs of life in the desert. Rather than the heavy, dark wood typical of the East, most of the furniture was made of light-colored material, some of it even whitewashed. Splashes of color were provided by rugs and pottery created by local Indians, a few of whom were friendly. The thick adobe walls provided protection from the blazing summer sun.

I was scrutinizing a painting of the local mountain range when Mandy returned from the barn. "Your home is unbelievable," I said.

"Are you wondering where I get the money to live in a place like this?" she asked with a smile.

"Oh, no! I just meant..."

What to say? I wanted to know *exactly* where and how she secured the money to maintain her extensive property in such pristine condition. Fortunately, she responded before I was compelled to risk a verbal blunder.

"I couldn't afford to keep this place going on my salary. I'm a widow. I get a very generous monthly check from a trust fund my husband left me."

"Oh. I'm sorry. I didn't realize—"

"You're sorry?" Mandy laughed. "Well, I'm not. I'm free, I'm independent, and I don't have to worry about money. I work because it suits me. I'm living my life exactly the way I want to live it."

"Then I'm happy for you. I really am."

"Thank you. Now, you must be starved. Let's see what we can put together for supper."

Since she hadn't been expecting company, she didn't have many supplies on hand. But we managed to assemble a passable stew made mostly from softened jerky and potatoes, which we supplemented with hardtack and a pot of hot coffee. By the time we finished cleaning up after the meal, the outside temperature had finally fallen below ninety degrees.


WE SAT IN the dark on the porch. I looked up at the sky and saw hundreds of stars that never showed themselves at home in St. Louis. The unfamiliar sounds of the desert's night creatures were somehow reassuring.

"I understand why you're so fond of the desert," I said. "It's so peaceful out here."

"I'm surprised you feel that way, considering what happened to you today. I mean, with the Fletchers dead and your job gone, that's quite unnerving." She paused in thought then added, "It must have been a hard trip, all the way out here from St. Louis."

"It wasn't as difficult as it would have been a few years ago. I took the train as far as Phoenix."

Mandy nodded. "Yes, since they opened up the southern route, it's much easier to get here." There was a hint of regret in her voice.

"Actually, the most unnerving part of the trip was the stagecoach ride here from the train station," I said with a smile.

She laughed. "That road is a nightmare if you're pulling a wagon. I prefer to ride Daisy into the city, although at her age that trail is far from her favorite."

In my plan I hadn't really considered how close we were to Phoenix. A rider on horseback could make the trip in a matter of hours. I resolved to avoid any discussion of my leaving Weaver's Flat.

"I don't know why I'm not more upset. I should be. But for some reason I feel quite comfortable here. Despite my world turning upside down, I have a feeling of well-being. I really can't explain it."

"In that case, the week will pass quickly for you. Tomorrow morning I'll walk into town. You can ride in on Daisy whenever you feel up to it, and we'll send that wire to your agency in St. Louis."

"I don't want you to have to walk to town. I've already put you to too much trouble."

"April, it's only a half mile." She leaned over and said in a stage whisper, "The only reason I ride in is to keep Daisy happy. She doesn't like to stay here alone all day. She wants to be with the other horses at the livery stable. She even gets kind of testy on my days off when she's stuck out here with nobody but me for company."

"And just how do you know this?" I couldn't suppress a chuckle. "Are you a horse mind reader?"

"No, but I can certainly understand them when they want me to. They know how to make their wishes quite clear, don't you think?"

I hesitated. "To tell you the truth, I don't know much about horses. I've ridden in coaches, of course. But I've never actually touched a horse, except for petting them on the snout a few times."

"You mean you've never even ridden a horse?"

"Not actually, no."

She leaned over and stared at her boots. "Okay. Okay. Let me think."

"Look, I don't have to go into town tomorrow. I'll just stay here. Maybe I can make myself useful. I could even cook us a nice supper for tomorrow evening." And I could avoid the problem of wiring the nonexistent agency in St. Louis.

She nodded. "All right. Tonight you can write your message to the placement agency, and I'll wire it to them in the morning."

"I'll work that out tomorrow while you're gone," I said. "There's no advantage to sending it right away."

As the hour grew late, I realized that there was only one bed in the house. If Mandy was uncomfortable about sharing it with me, she didn't show any sign of it. She wore one of her large work shirts to bed and fell asleep almost immediately.

I lay awake listening to her deep breathing and marveled at all that had happened so suddenly. After several days, the train had finally arrived in Phoenix. I had been fortunate to get a ride on the stagecoach after a wait of only a few hours. The modern age of transportation was truly overwhelming. Twenty-four hours earlier I had been on a train somewhere in New Mexico, heading west and hoping to locate a woman I had never met named Amanda Wells. And tonight that woman was sharing her bed with me.

MANDY BOUNDED OUT of bed at first light. After she and Daisy left, the house was quiet...too quiet. I decided that my time would best be spent in town, where I might pick up a thread to lead me to the information I sought. During the short walk to the post office, I became keenly aware of the sounds of the desert and of being observed by an unfamiliar assortment of living creatures. I stepped carefully along the ruts in the trail and arrived unscathed. I was glad I had gone in the morning before the heat became even more oppressive. The town was almost as quiet as Mandy's house, and it remained so for most of the day. With midsummer temperatures reaching well over a hundred degrees every day, only the most unavoidable activities were undertaken.

Around midday an old prospector brought in almost six ounces of gold nuggets. Mandy weighed them and placed them in a company container. She filled out the accompanying form with his name, the name and location of his claim, and the weight of the gold. He took the receipt she wrote out and went happily on his way up the street to Emery's where, he assured her, he intended to celebrate until the wee hours of the morning.

I went across the street to the meagerly stocked general store and bought a few basic supplies for Mandy's kitchen. We wouldn't be enjoying elaborate meals, but at least it would be an improvement over the makeshift supper we'd had the night before.

At four o'clock it was time to close for the day. Mandy locked up and we went up the street to the bank, where we dropped off the gold that had been brought in earlier for her to assay. From there we continued to the livery stable and picked up Daisy. Rather than burden the old horse with an extra rider, we walked home at a slow pace.

An illusion of peace and serenity surrounded Mandy. That is to say, I did not believe that it was possible for a woman to be as contented with her life as Mandy seemed to be, especially life in the isolated, uncivilized Arizona desert. Therefore, I concluded that my perception was an illusion, and I intended to find the reality that lay beneath. I intended to learn all about Amanda Wells, as well as her secret knowledge of the treasure known to be hidden in the nearby mountains.

When we reached the house, Mandy took Daisy to the barn to tend to her needs while I set to work in the kitchen. During the next hour I managed to prepare a supper that I judged to be passable and that Mandy swore was the best meal she had ever eaten.

We talked about the town as we ate. At one point Mandy joked about something that had happened at Emery's and we both laughed so hard that we had to stop eating. I had the sudden and unexpected realization that I was happier at that moment than I had been in years. A part of me wanted the world to stop moving forward right then and there, with the two of us exactly as we seemed to be. But the moment passed, and the complex reality of my situation settled over me once again.

Mandy said, "I was so distracted by all the post office business today, I forgot about the wire to your placement agency. I'll send it first thing tomorrow morning."

"Actually, I...I decided to write them a letter instead. The situation is too complicated to explain in a wire."

She put down her fork. "We have only one mail pickup per week. Any letters you write won't leave here until the stagecoach comes through next Tuesday."

"I know that."

"Yesterday you were upset about being stranded here for a week. I don't understand —"

"But that's not how I feel today." To my consternation, I realized that my planned deception had taken an unexpected turn. "There's something about...this place...that I'm drawn to. I feel comfortable here. And I'm not ready to make the trip all the way back to St. Louis. Not yet, anyway."

"Well then, there's no rush about getting that letter written. Any time during the next five days will do the trick." She picked up her fork and devoured the rest of her supper.


FOR THE NEXT few days I didn't go into town. I decided it would be fun to dress up the house instead. In the process, I thought I might even stumble upon some interesting information while Mandy was gone.

On the first morning, I brought some colorful cactus flowers and other desert blooms inside and placed them in bowls and cups in the main room. I put a gingham tablecloth that I had found stashed away in an old trunk on the dining room table and added a bouquet of wildflowers. I spent the afternoon preparing a supper that I hoped Mandy would enjoy. That evening, my efforts were rewarded with lavish praise. Mandy said the house had never looked so homey (she actually used that word—"homey") and as for the meal, I had outdone my efforts of the previous night. Her words sent a flush of pleasure through me.

In the following days, a pattern took shape. Mandy went to work every morning and returned in the evening to a hot supper and a house that began to feel more and more like a real home. I was thoroughly happy in the role I was playing.


ON SUNDAY WE packed a picnic basket with lunch and a bunch of carrots for Daisy and headed for the Superstition Mountains.

"I heard a story about a gold mine that's supposedly hidden here," I said as I spread out a blanket under the shade of a mesquite tree. "The 'Lost Dutchman Mine,' I think it was called."

Mandy laughed. "That tale gets weirder all the time. For one thing, the so-called Dutchman isn't Dutch. He's a German named Jacob Waltz, and he isn't lost. That conniving thief lives in Phoenix. If you want to meet him, you can just ask around next time you're down there."

"My understanding is that the mine is lost, not the Dutchman. The story I heard is that he comes up here a few times a year and mines enough gold to last him for several months."

"It isn't even a mine," Mandy said. "But he wants people to believe it is. He's got his reasons. He doesn't 'mine' the gold. He just takes it from the cache. It's the Peralta gold." She pulled a carrot from the sack sitting between us and took it to Daisy, who was tied loosely to a low-hanging mesquite branch.

"Well, I've never heard about that," I said with a shrug.

"Are you serious? Everybody in Arizona knows about the Peralta family."

I couldn't help but smile. "I see. I'm afraid that their fame hasn't spread east of the Mississippi River."

"I'm sorry, April. I've already come to think of you as a part of this place." She took a deep breath. "Okay, short version. Until a little over twenty years ago this area was a part of Mexico, and the Peralta family had an incredible amount of gold stashed in their mine here. Then under the Treaty of Guadalupe Hidalgo this became United States territory, including their mine of course, so they tried to move the gold south of the redefined Mexican border. In the process, they were ambushed and massacred by Apaches."

"That explains it," I said. "The only people who knew the location of the mine were killed. It's called a 'lost mine' because nobody knows where to find it, supposedly with the exception of the so-called Dutchman."

"Supposedly," said Mandy as she gazed absently at the Superstition Mountains.

I felt that she was on the brink of telling me what I had come all this way to learn. But then she seemed to lose interest in our conversation and she began to rummage through the picnic basket. On impulse, I decided to force the issue.

"Seth says the gold in that mine could be worth millions."

She looked up. "Who is Seth?"

"He's my fiancé. I expect to receive a letter from him soon."

The mention of Seth made me uneasy. I didn't understand why I felt that I was breaking some sort of bond that had formed between Mandy and me. But if the plan was to stay on course, Seth had to enter the picture soon.

For one thing, I needed to assure Mandy that the matter of the nonexistent placement agency in St. Louis was being handled. As the town's telegraph operator, she was privy to the contents of every incoming and outgoing wire. By exchanging letters with Seth, I could perpetuate the myth that he was dealing with the situation.

For another thing, I needed to provide a justification for my continued stay. Seth intended to leave his job in St. Louis and come to Weaver's Flat as soon as I had gotten enough information to move ahead with the plan.

Mandy turned back to the mountains. "Your fiancé. I see. I thought...I mean, you never mentioned —"

"He lives in St. Louis. He's thought quite a lot about moving to California or Arizona. Before I left, he talked about coming out here in a couple of months. If he likes it, we'll probably settle here when we get married." I was proceeding as planned. Still, I felt a stab of discomfort about it.

# Chapter Two

AS THE DAYS stretched into weeks, we settled into a routine. Mandy worked at the post office six days a week, while I took care of the cooking and household chores. I learned how to hitch Daisy to the wagon and ride into town for supplies. On Sundays Daisy would take us to various spots along the nearby creek for a picnic and change of scene.

We grew close, and sometimes we exchanged hugs and other gestures of affection. Having only my two brothers, I didn't have first-hand knowledge about the matter, but I imagined that this was how it felt to have a close relationship with a sister.

One night I had a bad dream. I awakened crying. Mandy awakened as well, and when she realized what had happened, she put her arms around me and assured me that everything was all right. Being given reassurance wasn't a new experience for me. My parents, grandmother, older brothers and an assortment of nannies had all comforted me many times and for many reasons over the course of my young life. It had usually placated me. Mandy's comforting reassurance did more. Inexplicably, I was exhilarated.

Although we knew it was temporary, we never discussed how or when the inevitable end of our arrangement would come. In the beginning, I had been edgy, anxious for Seth to arrive so that we could move ahead with our plan. But after a few weeks I became comfortable in a way I had never felt before, and eventually I wasn't at all occupied with when he would make his appearance.

Seth's letters began to arrive almost every week. Mandy brought them home and personally delivered them into my hands. The letter that would change everything came after five months. Seth wrote that he would arrive on the stagecoach three weeks hence. He wanted me to make arrangements for him. He needed a place to stay, preferably one that included meals. He knew that I was staying with Mandy and suggested that perhaps she had room for him as well.

I had no idea why I felt so angry. Anger, I had heard, was a mask for fear and/or pain. I forced myself to look deeper inside, and I realized that I felt both fear and pain with unexpected intensity. I felt violated in a way that I couldn't understand. I alternately paced the floor and flung myself on the couch, trying to suppress the urge to compose a wire to Seth, telling him not to come. I didn't know what was happening to me, and I couldn't bear to try to puzzle it out.

Mandy watched, uncomprehending, from the dining table. Finally she stood and came over to the couch, where I sat staring at the letter.

"Look, I think I can make room for him here," she said. "I can borrow a bed from Emery's and set up an area in the barn for him to sleep in."

"I suppose we'll have to do something like that," I said. Without thinking, I crushed the letter into a ball in my fist. *"Damn him!"*

"Whoa," Mandy gasped. "I thought you were looking forward to this."

"Well...of course I am. It's just that...I'm not certain anymore of what I want. I'm ambivalent about certain matters. I wish he weren't coming so soon." I was surprised to hear myself express those thoughts aloud.

THREE WEEKS LATER, on the day Seth was scheduled to arrive, Mandy and I took the wagon into town. With only an hour to wait, we left Daisy and the wagon in front of the post office. The stagecoach arrived on schedule and deposited Seth at the front door. Ignoring his passenger, Amos brought in the mail from Phoenix.

"Howdy, Mandy." Turning to me he added, "April." He put the incoming mail sack on the counter, stashed a single small, heavy wooden crate under his left arm, and hoisted the outgoing sack next to it onto his right shoulder. "Judging from the weight of the mail, I'd say everybody in town wrote a letter or two this week."

Mandy looked past him to the young man who stood on the sidewalk outside. "It appears that our esteemed visitor has arrived," she said.

"Yeah, he's 'esteemed' all right," Amos muttered. "Beggin' your pardon, April. I know he's a friend of yours, but I swear, if those Eastern dudes think they're so much better'n us, I wonder why they don't just stay put back there and leave us alone."

"Did he give you a hard time?" Mandy asked.

"Been trying to order me around like I'm his personal servant all the way from Phoenix." He shrugged. "I guess he's your problem now. Says he's engaged to marry you, April, and he'll be staying with you out at Mandy's place."

Mandy nodded. "I borrowed a bed from Emery's. I'm letting him sleep in my barn while he's here."

Amos roared with laughter. "You'd better keep your doors locked, Mandy. That Eastern dandy won't last even one night sleeping in a barn. And you'd better hope he never finds out what that bed's been through." He glanced at me and said, "Sorry, April."

Mandy grinned. "I appreciate learning something about my house guests ahead of time. Thanks for the advice."

Moments after the stagecoach pulled away, I stepped outside. Seth folded me in his arms. Releasing me after a moment, he glared at Daisy then tossed his suitcase onto the wagon. When he started to climb up to the seat, I stopped him and told him he needed to come into the post office for an introduction to his hostess.

He followed me inside. I sensed right away that Mandy knew my joyful demeanor was forced. I didn't really care.

"Mandy, this is Seth Thompson, my...this is Seth." I turned to him. "And this is Amanda Wells. Mandy. She's a friend of mine."

Something almost menacing in my tone must have alerted Seth to the possibility that the original plan might have been altered. When we had worked it out in St. Louis, it was agreed that I would arrive alone and ingratiate myself to Amanda Wells. Now I was quite fiercely protective of her. He looked at me curiously.

Seth had learned of Amanda's existence and her knowledge of the secrets of the Superstition Mountains from the Fletcher boys. When their parents were killed in the fire that destroyed the family home outside of Weaver's Flat, the brothers, aged twelve and thirteen, were sent to live with their mother's sister and her husband in St. Louis. There they were enrolled in the Braddock Academy, where they would prepare for college.

In his capacity as coach of most of the athletic teams at Braddock, Seth heard many of the brothers' tales of the unsettled Arizona Territory. One particular story fascinated him. Typical of such stories, it involved a secret gold mine supposedly worth millions. But in the case of the so-called Lost Dutchman Mine, many people had actually seen some of the gold taken from it by an eccentric recluse known as the Dutchman who went to great lengths to keep its location secret. Nobody knew exactly where the mine was, with the possible exception of the notably tight lipped Amanda Wells.

Seth researched the Lost Dutchman Mine. As far as he could ascertain, it was real, it was rich, and its location was the best-kept secret in Arizona. Our fantasies of unlimited riches led to wildly irrational ideas, and finally to an elaborate scheme. Together, Seth and I developed a plan to locate the mine and claim its wealth for ourselves.

Now that he was finally here in Arizona in the presence of Amanda Wells for the first time, he turned on the charm.

"It's a pleasure to meet you, Amanda. I'm very grateful that you have room for me at your ranch."

"I'm afraid it doesn't amount to much," she said with a shrug. "We just cleared out a corner and set up a bed for you in the barn..."

"The barn? You're putting me up in your barn?" His face flushed.

I tugged at his sleeve. "It isn't as bad as it sounds, Seth. Wait until you see the arrangement. I don't think you'll be upset at all." I dropped my arm and took a small step back when he glared at me.

"All right," he growled. "Let's go and have a look." He spun around and pulled me after him.

"I'll see you two this evening," Mandy called as we reached the front door.

Seth climbed into the wagon next to me. I picked up the reins and made the usual clicking sound with my teeth. Daisy bobbed her head slightly, then eased forward, pulled the wagon around, and set out for home.

"You've done well," Seth began. "I never imagined you would end up living with the woman"

"As it happens, there was nowhere else for me to go. The only place in town that rents rooms is Emery's. If I were a man, I could have stayed there. But since it's mainly a saloon and house of ill repute..."

"Oh, good grief." He shook his head in disgust. "You're telling me that the only places to stay in this town are Amanda's barn and the local bordello?"

I couldn't help smiling. "That's just the way it is here, Seth."


INSIDE MANDY'S BARN, Seth pulled me into an embrace. I melted into his arms in anticipation of the feeling of closeness I had missed for the past five months. And I felt nothing at all. I drew back abruptly, surprised and confused.

He cocked his head. "What's wrong, little lady?"

It was a valid question that I was unable to answer. A man who had once captivated my heart now left me feeling lukewarm at best. What had happened? My mind flashed over the events of my life since I had last seen Seth. I had boarded the train in St. Louis at the beginning of our grand scheme to secure the treasure in gold, rumored to be worth millions, hidden in the Superstition Mountains of Arizona. After my arrival in Phoenix, the stagecoach had brought me to Mandy...no, I corrected myself, not to Mandy. No. The stagecoach had brought me to Weaver's Flat.

What, then, had happened to me in Weaver's Flat that had somehow eradicated my intense feelings for Seth? There was the little town itself, of course. The merchants, the prospectors, even the ladies at Emery's had been considerate and kind to me. And there was Mandy, who had welcomed me into a world I had not known existed.

I had learned about living in the desert and maintaining a ranch. My life with Mandy was uncomplicated and fulfilling. Wonderful, sweet Mandy. The idea of deceiving her, I suddenly realized, had become unthinkable. I loved Mandy and....

"April!" I came back to the moment when he shook me angrily. "My God, woman, what's wrong with you?"

"I'm not certain," I whispered. "I mean, nothing is wrong, exactly. But something is different."

He tightened his grip on my shoulders. "Look, I don't give a damn what's the same or what's different. Now tell me what you know."

In that moment, my entire world seemed suddenly to shift. I took a deep breath and plunged in. "I'm sorry, Seth. I can't do this. I'm sorry it went so far before I realized it. I can't deceive Mandy. And I can't marry you."

He shoved me. I fell backwards, landing hard against the rear wagon wheel. I looked up at him in disbelief.

His face was crimson. "Have you gone mad?"

"No, but I think you may have," I said shakily. I was shocked and angry and scared and I hoped that I wasn't going to cry. "I think it best that you forget about the plan. And everything else, for that matter."

"Fine, you miserable bitch. Consider it done."

He jumped on the wagon and, finding no whip, screamed at Daisy while yanking sharply on the reins. I watched in horror as he forced the old horse into a gallop toward town.


I RAN AFTER them. Ten minutes later, I found the rig outside of Emery's. I led Daisy to the livery stable, where the terrified horse would receive prompt attention. Then I walked to the post office.

Mandy was surprised when I entered.

"I didn't expect to see you before I got home this evening," she said. "Did you leave Seth there by himself?"

I didn't know what to say. I could tell her quite truthfully that I had not left Seth alone at the ranch. I could add that Seth was in fact at Emery's, probably either drinking or renting a room, or perhaps even renting a woman.

I could tell her quite truthfully that Seth was no longer my fiancé. I could add that we had separated because I couldn't go through with our scheme to deceive her. I could confess that I couldn't bring myself to tease certain information out of her about the whereabouts of other people's wealth, thereby making myself unimaginably rich.

What would she do if I told her everything? I deserved to be thrown out of her home. I deserved for her to despise me for the hurtful deception I had perpetrated. I couldn't bear the thought of the pain it would bring her. Nor could I bear the thought of ending the life I had with Mandy. So I lied to her.

"I suppose that five months apart can change your view of a person. Seth doesn't feel the same about me as he did before. And truth be told, my feelings for him have changed as well." That much was true. I looked at the floor and continued. "He's decided not to stay at the ranch. I suppose he'll head back to St. Louis as soon as possible."

Mandy was trying to frown, and doing a poor job of it. "He'll have to stay at Emery's until he can find a way out of here."

I hadn't thought of that. The stagecoach wouldn't be back for a week, so unless he could arrange another way out, Seth was stranded. It was unsettling to think of him staying in town. As it stood at that moment, he was ready to abandon the plan altogether and leave Weaver's Flat. But if he couldn't leave for several days, his inevitable poking and prodding might lead him to some bit of information that would tempt him to stay. I wanted him out of town and out of my life as soon as possible.

Since the post office was due to close in less than two hours, I decided to stay there with Mandy. For one thing, I didn't want to take a chance on encountering Seth. For another thing, I wanted to give Daisy time to settle down after her unpleasant experience. With Mandy at the reins, she would be comfortable pulling the wagon home.

Hank Edwards, one of the barkeeps at Emery's, came in a few minutes before closing to post a letter. Hank was compact and muscular, and although he was probably in his thirties, his dark, leathery skin gave him the appearance of an older man. He lived in one of the rooms above the bar and kept to himself for the most part. He was seemingly unaffected by the brothel activities, fist fights, brawls, holdups, gun fights and murders that were regular occurrences at Emery's. Despite his surroundings, Hank was a gentleman whenever ladies were present. He and Mandy were friends.

Hank didn't see me at first. He gave Mandy his letter and paid for the stamp. She tossed it in the pouch and asked, "How are things at Emery's today?"

"That young man of April's surely does have an angry bee in his bonnet. Came in this afternoon acting like the King of Prussia, demanding to rent the best room in the house."

Mandy laughed. "The best room in the house? What's that supposed to mean?"

"Beats me," he said. "Nobody else knew either. Martha Mae thought maybe he was making reference to the ladies and went to introduce herself. Well, long story short, that's not what he had in mind. I guess with April in the picture—"

With that, I burst out of the back room. "Hank, I want to make two things clear. First, Seth Thompson is not 'my young man.' Second, I am not 'in the picture.' As of today, Seth and I are no longer engaged to be married. Nor will we ever be again."

To my surprise, he jumped back. "Beggin' your pardon, April. I didn't realize you were here."

"Did he rent a room at Emery's?" I asked. I wanted assurance that he would not return to Mandy's barn later, expecting to sleep there.

"Yep. Rented a room, then started asking around about where he could buy a horse."

Mandy frowned. "A horse? Why would he want to buy a horse? He led April to believe that he wants to leave Weaver's Flat as soon as he can."

"Beats me, Mandy. Maybe he intends to ride it to Phoenix and sell it there."

"That doesn't make sense." She shook her head. "He'd lose too much money doing that. The market for horses down there is terrible. They've got more than they need."

He shrugged. "Maybe he doesn't know that. Anyway, he's lookin' to buy a horse for some reason." He turned to the door. "I gotta get back. See ya' later, Mandy." He glanced at me and added, "April."

"Why would he want to buy a horse?" Mandy muttered.

"Perhaps he just wants to ride it to Phoenix," I said. "Perhaps it's just because he doesn't want to wait until next week for the stagecoach." I hoped I was correct, but I had a bad feeling in the pit of my stomach.

"Perhaps." Mandy was clearly concerned. "Perhaps."

SHE BARELY SPOKE for the rest of the day. That evening at supper, she finally said what was on her mind.

"I believe that Seth wants to remain here to try to win you back. That's why he wants to buy a horse. He thinks he'll be here for awhile."

If Seth really didn't plan to leave, I knew it had nothing to do with me. I decided to tell Mandy what I suspected. "If he does stay, it isn't because of me," I said. It made me uncomfortable, but I continued. "Seth hopes to find the Lost Dutchman Mine. He thinks you know where it is."

She glared at me. "Why does he believe that?"

She was angry, and it frightened me. "He didn't hear it from me," I said. My voice trembled despite my best effort to remain calm.

I stated the facts, but changed the order in which I had learned them. Painful as it was, I pressed on. "I've heard whispers around town. Not much, because people know that we live together, so when they see that I'm within earshot, they stop."

"And what are they whispering about?" she growled.

"People say you could never afford this ranch on your salary from the post office. They wonder about your dead husband, if he ever really existed. There's no other source of money that you have access to." I wanted to stop there. I wanted to cry. But I forced myself to continue. "They know about your love/hate relationship with old Jacob Waltz. They know you take Daisy into the mountains for a few days every now and then. It all adds up to one nasty rumor. And Seth is aware of every bit of it."

"I see," she said, clearly stunned that so much was known or had been surmised about her personal life.

I felt horrible for hurting Mandy, but at the same time I was relieved that the truth was out in the open. Still, if she thought about it, she would realize that my appearance in her life had to be connected to what she supposedly knew about the Lost Dutchman Mine. And at that point it would be easy to deduce that Seth and I had colluded to deceive her. I hoped she would see that in revealing my secret, I was abandoning my part in the shameful scheme. But it turned out not to be so simple.

Mandy wouldn't look at me for the rest of the evening. We didn't speak at all. After she blew out the candle at bedtime, she didn't give me the sisterly caresses that had become our nightly habit. Instead of falling asleep in her arms, as I had done every night for over a month, I lay alone on my side of the bed. I stared into the dark for hours, pondering the mess I had made of my life. In one day I had alienated the only two people that mattered to me: Seth and Mandy.

But Seth didn't matter to me at all anymore. The way his mind worked, his behavior, and his total lack or concern for anyone else, disgusted me. Earlier in the day I had found for the first time that his physical presence disgusted me as well. All I wanted from Seth was for him to be gone.

But Mandy mattered, although I couldn't pinpoint exactly why she seemed to be the focal point of my life. And now with my clumsy confession, I had driven her away from me, probably forever.

Everything was so mixed up.

# Chapter Three

THE NEXT MORNING, Mandy was in the barn getting Daisy ready when Seth appeared on a large black horse.

"Get your things, April," he demanded.

He offered no hello, not even a kind word. He issued a command as if he owned me and could take me away from Mandy merely because he wished to.

"We concluded this discussion yesterday," I said. "I think I made myself quite clear. The plan is off. Our engagement is off. I'm not going back to St. Louis with you."

"Oh, but you are." His face twisted with anger. "You and your big mouth ruined my plan to get my hands on that gold. But I still owe it to you to take you out of this godforsaken place. And that is precisely what I intend to do."

At that moment, Mandy led Daisy out of the barn. She wore a stoic expression. When she looked at Seth, it didn't change.

I don't know if she saw Seth's body stiffen when he saw her, but it was obvious to me. Even the big black horse jerked nervously, and Daisy nickered. Suddenly the atmosphere was charged with danger, as though something horrendous was happening, and it was all the more frightening because nobody knew what it was.

"I'm taking April," said Seth.

Mandy's eyes didn't leave his. She spoke softly. "If that's what she wants."

No, it wasn't what I wanted, and I had no intention of letting Seth or anyone else decide my fate. Mandy was still upset with me because of what I had told her the previous night. But I was certain that she would support me if I stood my ground.

I looked Seth in the eye and said, "I'm staying with Mandy."

"So that's how it is," he said with a sneer. "You and Mandy have a little love nest here, eh?"

"I'll tell you this much, Seth. Mandy is honest. She doesn't scheme and lie to people. I respect her for that. And, yes, I suppose you could say that I love her for it. It's a refreshing change from...other people."

His eyes flared. He jumped from his horse and lunged at me. He grabbed my arm so roughly that my dress tore open at the seam of my sleeve. Mandy moved as fast as lightning. Suddenly her hand was on my other arm and the barrel of her pistol was jammed under Seth's chin.

She spoke slowly, her voice low, exaggerating every syllable. "Let go of April. Get on your horse and leave. If you ever set foot on this property again, I will kill you."

Although I had never heard her speak of violence, I believed her. Apparently Seth did too, because he turned pale and did exactly as he was told. We watched him until he disappeared from sight.

From that point on, I was afraid to stay at the ranch by myself. If Seth found out that Mandy had gone into town alone, he would come for me. He seemed to have no reservations about taking me against my will and forcing me to leave Weaver's Flat. I could understand his frustration with me for ruining the plan. But I could see that something else was going on in his mind — something more sinister that I didn't understand.

"I think you'd best come into town with me today," Mandy said.

I nodded. We went to the barn and hitched Daisy to the wagon. Then we rode to town in silence.


IT WAS BUSINESS as usual. There was no sign of Seth or the big black horse. I found myself hoping that he had left for Phoenix and would never return. But it was not to be.

Just before noon, Martha Mae Kellogg, one of the women who worked at Emery's, burst through the back door of the post office. To my surprise, she was nervous and maybe even frightened. She went directly to Mandy.

"Seth Thompson is over at the bar, and he's already drunk," she said.

Mandy shrugged. "Seth and I had an altercation this morning. He's probably still upset."

"More than upset. More than that." She grabbed Mandy's sleeve. "He's telling everybody that you're a tom and you went after April...and that you and April are lovers."

"It isn't true. We aren't lovers," Mandy said.

"That's not the point. If they find out that we —"

"Shut up, Martha Mae!"

They both glanced at me, and in that instant my world stood still. A thousand thoughts raced through my mind. Some of the pieces of the puzzle that I had not understood fell into place, but at the same time I realized that the puzzle itself was much more complex than I had imagined.

Most confusing of all were my own emotions. I had known and readily acknowledged that I loved Mandy. I had welcomed the physical closeness that had become part of our relationship. Suddenly it all took on a different meaning. Martha Mae spun on her heel and rushed out the door, leaving us in silence.

There was nowhere I could go to be alone, to think. But that was just as well, because I was afraid to face what had happened. Mandy said nothing, and I didn't know if she was looking at me, because I couldn't bring myself to look in her direction.

After a few minutes, the telegraph machine started to clatter, and Mandy went to the desk to transcribe the incoming message. That seemed to break the spell.

We spent the rest of the afternoon doing the usual office work and conducting business with the people who came in. Although the atmosphere was charged, we both persisted in pretending that nothing had happened. It wasn't until the evening during supper that Mandy finally broke our awkward silence.

"April, I'm such a fool," she said. "I don't know how I imagined this would end. I guess I never allowed myself to think about it. I only know that I'm in love with you." She looked at the floor. "I'm such a fool."

A part of me wasn't certain what I felt or what I wanted, and was afraid to find out. Another part of me, deeper within, knew the answer. And the truth terrified me. Mandy's feelings for me didn't repel me. They drew me closer to her.

"You're not a fool," I told her. "When I first met you, I believed that I could play you for a fool. But after I got to know you, everything changed."

"What about...what about all the gossip at Emery's? Aren't you worried about where it will lead?"

"I'm worried about us, Mandy. I don't know where we're headed together."

"Maybe it's time we found out," she said. She pulled me up from my chair and took me in her arms.

She kissed me in a way she never had before. It was a lover's kiss. My entire body came alive with excitement. I felt intense heat in my abdomen. I wanted something very badly, and I couldn't identify exactly what it was. But my instinct told me that Mandy could give me what I needed. After a blissful few moments she withdrew.

"Come to bed and let me pleasure you," she whispered.

Like dancers locked in embrace, we guided each other to bed. My heart pounded as we undressed together. I was as frightened as I had ever been in my life, but nothing in the world could have changed my desire to continue.

I lay on my back, naked, with no idea of what to expect. Then Mandy was with me, covering my body with hers. She explored me with her hands and mouth. I was filled with pleasure, coupled with an intense longing I couldn't identify — like an itch that I didn't know how to scratch. But in the next few minutes, it all became clear.

When she brushed against my inner thigh, rational thought became impossible. My mind simply switched off and my body took command. Her fingers moved inside of me, stroking, stroking, stroking, while her thumb moved expertly over the center of my longing. Suddenly I felt an overwhelming pleasure more intense than I had ever imagined possible. I clasped Mandy to me and cried out in ecstasy as my first sexual climax washed over me.

I caught my breath and looked at Mandy's face. Her eyes were filled with love, and something else that I now recognized as desire. I wanted nothing more than to fulfill that desire, but I didn't know where to begin. She showed me.

With soft whispers and gentle movements, she made me understand what she needed. I was exhilarated by the feeling of Mandy pressed against me, feeling the reverberations pulse through her body as I brought her to orgasm. Even before she recovered I was fully aroused. With my eyes and my body, I begged her to take me again.

We made love all night long. It was just before dawn when I first became aware that this new hunger of mine could actually be sated, if only for a few hours, or maybe in the future for a day or so. I needed sleep.

In a perfect world, it would have been Sunday and we could have stayed in bed all day. But it was Friday, and Mandy was expected in town, and I wasn't about to leave her side. Reluctantly, we rose to face the day.

ON THE WAY to town, I began to understand the implications of what was happening. My sympathetic feelings toward Seth were rapidly diminishing. He had been my first lover. He had never made any attempt to satisfy me. In fact, although I knew about orgasms, I had assumed that only men had them. Now I knew differently.

Without realizing it, I had acknowledged my feelings for Mandy and the nature of our relationship to Seth the previous day, before we had even consummated our love. Now his reaction made sense to me. I was certain that there was trouble ahead for Mandy and me. But I didn't anticipate how much.

As the morning crawled by, I couldn't get my mind off the delightful anticipation of what lay ahead when we went home for the evening. But my thoughts were interrupted when Martha Mae Kellogg slipped through the back door in the same manner as she had the day before.

"Seth Thompson has gotten worse," she said. "He's completely out of control now. He says you threatened to kill him yesterday."

Mandy nodded. "It's true. I did do that. He came out to the ranch and started to bother April and—"

"Because April is your lover, that's what he says. Because you're afraid that he's going to take your lover away from you." She clenched her fists. "They're starting to believe him, too."

"I can't do much about that, Martha Mae. We'll just have to wait until he runs out of steam."

"You don't understand. There's more to the talk than just you and April." She slapped her hand on the counter. "Some of the men remember how a few of us get together occasionally for the charity circle. They're starting to wonder."

A flash of anger crossed Mandy's face, then quickly became a worried frown. Whatever they were talking about, I felt that they, or at least Mandy, owed me an explanation.

"What about the charity circle?" I demanded.

Mandy took a deep breath and plunged in. "There's a group. Four of the women from Emery's, three ranch wives, and me. We get together every month or so to do some work for a couple of charities down in Phoenix. It doesn't amount to much—preserving a little food, sewing a few shirts—"

"And slipping out for a quick tryst with the lady of our choice," Martha Mae said.

Mandy glared at her. "It's the only thing some of those women live for. They're not hurting anyone. As long as nobody learns of their activities, they won't be hurt either."

"That's just the point, dammit," Martha Mae screamed. "Last night at the bar their conversation started to drift around to the charity circle. Seth's ears pricked up right away. Luckily, Belle and I overheard, and we managed to distract them from the discussion." She took a step toward Mandy. "But I'm telling you, it's just a matter of time. The girls from Emery's can move on; there will always be a place for us. But the ranch wives—their lives would be ruined, with no hope of salvation."

Mandy perched on the desk and looked at the floor. "You're right," she said softly. "And I'm to blame. I was a fool to think I could live like this forever."She looked at me and said, "I love you. And I have to get out of Weaver's Flat. Will you come with me?"

Living without Mandy was unthinkable. I answered without hesitation. "Yes, I will."

Martha Mae went back to Emery's, relieved that Mandy and I planned to leave town and hopeful that Seth, fueled by his humiliation and anger, would follow. Only then could life in Weaver's Flat, complete with the charity circle, return to normal.

Mandy was quiet and thoughtful for the rest of the afternoon. I envisioned figurative little gears turning in her head as she worked out the details of our move. I didn't know where she planned to take us or how we would survive. As it turned out, I would not have believed it anyway.


AFTER AN ETERNITY, it was time to close for the day. We fetched Daisy and the wagon, and headed home. When we approached the barn, Daisy uncharacteristically jerked her head up and sniffed the air.

Mandy seemed to tense up. She jumped off the wagon and opened the barn door as usual. When she came back, she put a finger to her lips, indicating that I shouldn't speak. She led Daisy into the barn and stopped short of the usual spot. She signaled me to stay seated on the wagon. Then she climbed the ladder into the loft.

After a moment, the silence was broken by a rustling sound. With Mandy nowhere in sight, Seth apparently assumed that she had left the barn. He emerged from behind some bales of hay and confronted me. He was seething.

"You've shamed me, April. You've ruined my life and you've shamed me."

"I've done nothing to you, Seth. You have no reason to do anything to me. I just want you to leave me alone."

He screamed, "Not after what you've done. I could have you committed, you know. That's what happens to wives who become perverts."

He was either well on his way to going insane, or already there. I had never seen him like this, and it frightened me. But I was determined to stand up to him, regardless of the consequences.

I reiterated my position yet again. "I'll tell you one more time. I am not your wife. I will never be your wife. Our engagement has ended. Whatever was between us is over. I don't know how to make that any clearer."

"No!" he shrieked.

In the next moment, events moved so quickly that I couldn't entirely absorb what was happening. Seth reached for me. Mandy appeared from above. Clinging to a rope she had tied to a rafter, she flew through the air feet first. Her boot made direct contact with Seth's jaw before he even realized she was there. He let out a grunt and crumpled.

Mandy dropped to the ground. She tied his hands behind his back with two strips of rawhide. Then she turned him over to see if he was alive. He was.

"We need to get him back to town," she said through clenched teeth.

"When people see what you did to him, they might tend to take his view of the situation," I said.

She shook her head. "Not when they find out he attacked you. People around here don't take kindly to men who assault women." She frowned and added, "White women."

Seth was semiconscious when we loaded him into the wagon. We hauled him back to Emery's. Mandy went inside and came out a minute later, accompanied by two burly looking men with long hair and heavy beards. They were local prospectors who had found a fairly rich vein of silver nearby and had used part of their new-found fortune to pay for room and board at Emery's.

"I think his jaw is broken," Mandy told them. "I'll make sure that Doc Hudson has a look at it when he comes through next week."

"How did it happen?" one of the men asked.

"I did it. He came to the ranch and assaulted April. She tried to fight him off, and I lent her a hand. It was self-defense."

The man scowled at Seth. "This Eastern dandy has a habit of upsetting women. Martha Mae and Belle were ready to scratch his eyes out, just last night."

"Don't know what his problem is," the other man added, "but he surely seems to want to stir up trouble of some sort."

Mandy said, "Beats me, Caleb. Anyway, it appears that he's going to be confined to his room for a few days. Probably won't be able to move his jaw. Probably won't be able to talk." She leaned over and peered at Seth's swollen face. "Tell Hank to bring milk and soup to his room a couple of times a day. And a straw."

She straightened up and looked at both men. "I'll keep his horse at my place until he's well enough to ride again."

The men lifted Seth off the wagon and carried him into Emery's. It was almost dark when we headed home for the second time that day.


I EXPECTED THE dreadful events of the day to have a negative effect on our lovemaking that night, but they didn't. Maybe we needed an escape from the emotional stress that Seth had caused. Maybe we just needed more physical pleasure, more sexual release, more time in the paradise we had found in each other. My apprehension of the previous night was gone. I knew precisely what I wanted from Mandy. I knew where and how I wanted her to touch me. And I knew precisely what she wanted from me. It was more intense, more fervid, more passionate, and it was wonderful.

It had been dark for a couple of hours before I was finally overcome by exhaustion. My complete lack of sleep the night before was beginning to take its toll. I fell back on the bed and stared numbly at the ceiling. The candle Mandy had lit flickered and burned out. The darkness changed my mood.

"What are we going to do?" I asked.

"Don't worry, we'll be just fine." She kissed my cheek and whispered, "Goodnight, my love."

# Chapter Four

"WAKE UP, APRIL," whispered a distant voice.

I opened my eyes and gazed at Mandy — not so distant after all. I looked toward the window.

"It's barely light. We can sleep a little longer." I pulled the blanket over my head.

She pulled it back. "No, we have to get up now. We're going on a trip, and we'll need every bit of daylight."

"We can't go anywhere today. It's Saturday. You have to work."

She shook her head. "I'm not going to work today. I'll stop by and leave a note on the door. Whatever business there is will have to wait until Monday. We have something important to do. We have to get started right now."

I struggled out of bed and started to pull on my dress. She stopped me and gave me a pair of her buckskin trousers to wear instead. It was then I learned that Daisy would not be pulling us in the wagon as usual, but carrying me on her back. Mandy would ride Seth's big black horse, which she told me was a "spirited but manageable gelding called Bingo," and we were going into the depths of the Superstition Mountains.

We packed an abundance of water, a blanket and very little else. The horses might find a few edible plants, but we would have nothing to eat. We took extra saddlebags, which were empty. Mandy said we needed as much empty space as possible; they would be full and very heavy when we returned.

Although Daisy and I were friends, she seemed as uncomfortable as I was at the prospect of having me on her back. I still had never ridden a horse, and I think Daisy knew it. Mandy shushed both of us and hoisted me up into the saddle. Once settled, we accepted the inevitable.

We stopped at the post office on our way out. The town was still asleep. Mandy tacked a note on the door stating that business would resume on Monday. We continued through town and turned toward the mountains.

An hour later, we reached the base of the Superstitions. We followed the trail for a few miles, until it forked. Mandy stopped. I didn't think she had forgotten which branch of the fork to follow, but she was hesitant. She dismounted and told me to do the same.

"The horses smell something," she said. She scrutinized the rocks that surrounded us." Someone is nearby."

We left the trail and hiked up the base of a small hill, drawing the horses behind us. We found a rock formation that hid us from the view of the trail and waited. In a few minutes, the horses' nostrils flared while they made noises that indicated another animal was near. Then we heard the brae of a mule. Mandy climbed up one of the rocks to see what she could, then scrambled down quickly.

"It's a mule by itself. It must have broken loose from somewhere around here. It's heading toward town."

"Does that mean someone got there ahead of us — wherever we're going?" I asked.

She shook her head. "That's doubtful. Most likely there's a prospector up there wondering how his mule broke loose." She grinned. "Wait here. I'll go down and catch it and tie it up. We'll take it with us."

"Isn't that horse stealing? Or mule stealing, or something? Can't you get into a lot of trouble for that?" I asked.

"You bet you can," she said. "But we're not stealing. We're rescuing. After that mule brings back an extra load of gold, I'll take it to the livery stable and report it found. Maybe I'll even get a reward," she said with a laugh as she ran back toward the trail.

Then it hit me what she had said — *an extra load of gold*. So the rumor that had spread all the way to St. Louis was true: the Lost Dutchman Mine really did exist, and a woman named Amanda Wells really did know where it was located.

Six months ago, that knowledge would have thrilled me. I would have been eager to trick the woman into revealing the whereabouts of the mine for my own purposes. How my life had changed! The knowledge still thrilled me, because now that woman was the greatest love of my life and we were about to run away together with a fortune.

Secured with a lead rope, the mule was reasonably cooperative and slowed our pace only slightly. I recognized Weaver's Needle from a photograph I had seen on exhibit at the museum in St. Louis. We continued in a southeast direction to a place called Needle Canyon. We were surrounded by huge formations of rocks weighing thousands of tons each. Many of them were precariously perched on other rocks and looked so unstable that I wondered if they might tumble down and crush us to death in the next few moments. But Mandy said they had been like that for as long as anybody could remember, so they weren't likely to fall down just then.

There were hundreds of tall, narrow gaps between the huge rocks. Mandy headed directly to one of them. It looked like all the others — surrounded by large boulders, smaller rocks and a variety of plants struggling to survive on a few drops of water and an occasional flash flood.

We secured the animals. Mandy removed the lantern from her pack and led me to an obscure opening. She lit the lantern and I followed her.

Inside was a big, empty cave. I thought she must have lost her bearings somehow. The stacks of gold that I had anticipated were nowhere to be seen. In fact, the cave was completely empty, except for a few large rocks and the skeleton of some long dead creature of the desert. I started to move back toward the cave opening.

Mandy stopped me. "Don't worry. There's nothing in here to be afraid of."

"But we're in the wrong place. This isn't—"

She laughed. "That's exactly what you're supposed to believe. But we're just about there."

She slipped three metal bars from their hiding place beneath the skeleton. I had read about the power of leverage in various scientific publications. Now I saw Mandy put it to use. She moved one bar, then another, alternately prying and holding various portions of a large boulder. After about three minutes, the rock lay next to a twenty-inch opening on the floor of the cave. She looked up and winked at me.

Several flat-sided rocks were arranged to serve as stairs. We backed down them, as we would on a ladder, until we reached the floor of a subterranean room. Mandy held the lantern up and turned slowly around the room. I had never seen so much gold in my life.

It wasn't in the form of bars or coins, as I was accustomed to seeing. It was embedded in small chunks of rock. Mandy told me that in remote, inaccessible places like the Superstition Mountains, it wasn't possible to haul out great quantities of unrefined ore, the way they did in open pit mines with nearby railroad cars. The rocks surrounding us had been crushed and hand-sorted where they were found. Only the highest grade ore was removed from hard-to-reach locations.

"But why did they hide it here?" I asked. "Why didn't they take it out when they found it?"

Mandy said, "Nobody knows for sure that this gold actually came from around here. Some people think the Peralta family used the Superstition Mountains the way you and I use a bank. They might have deposited their gold here for safekeeping, while this was still Mexican land."

The story of the Peralta family was well known in Weaver's Flat. While moving their considerable fortune to Mexico from the newly acquired Arizona Territory, they had been massacred by hostile Apache Indians.

Every part of the legend of the lost gold was frightening to me. So much had been at stake, and there had been so much violence. I had a strong feeling that the story wasn't over, and I was apprehensive about it.

"Where do we fit into this?" I asked Mandy. "How did we come to be standing here right now?"

"That's a complicated story. But you'll understand everything once we get to Phoenix and you meet a couple of people there." She looked around the cavern and said, "Meanwhile, we have to get to work."


WE SPENT THE rest of the day carrying gold ore up from the

subterranean room to the opening of the cave, where it would remain hidden until the next morning. When we had brought up enough to fill our saddlebags, Mandy maneuvered the boulder back over the opening and replaced the metal bars under the skeleton. We had barely made a dent in the huge stock of ore.

It was almost dark by the time we finished. We set up a rough camp a few hundred yards from the cave, but didn't light a fire for fear of drawing attention to ourselves. I didn't sleep well. The hard ground was uncomfortable. The blazing heat of the desert disappeared, but it grew cold after a few hours, and our blanket didn't do much good.

I listened to the sounds of the desert. Mandy had assured me that the horses would warn us of approaching danger, such as a rattlesnake, but I was apprehensive. I stared up at the stars and waited for the hours to pass.

At last daylight began to appear in the eastern sky. Mandy stirred and sat up, apparently fully rested. We saddled the animals. It took over an hour to carry the gold ore from the mouth of the cave and fill the saddlebags. Although we would be on foot, we knew the weight would be challenging for the animals. With such a heavy load, they would have to travel slowly.

THE RETURN TRIP was difficult. Although it was a relatively cool day, the animals were sweating, and we had to stop every hour or so to give them shade, rest and water.

At last Weaver's Flat came into view. We used an old cattle trail to circle around the town. It wouldn't do for anyone to see our little caravan with its heavy cargo. It was a relief to reach the safety of the ranch by late afternoon. We unloaded the saddle bags and stashed their contents behind some bales of hay. The animals recovered quickly, once we tended to their needs.

We were tired, hungry and dirty. We walked down to the little creek that ran through the end of the property, where there were shallow pools with enough fresh water for bathing. Mandy stripped, unconcerned that anyone might be nearby. I was hesitant, but I followed her lead and quickly forgot my apprehension. We took more time than we needed, basking in the joy of the cool, refreshing water and the sight of each other.

It was early evening when we returned to the house to prepare supper. We were too tired to cook a proper meal, so we settled for part of a slab of salt-cured ham, a pot of beans and some dried figs. We washed it all down with a pot of Mandy's dreadfully strong coffee.

At last it was bedtime. The consuming passion of our newfound love was only slightly tempered by our exhaustion. Lovemaking and sleep battled and alternately prevailed until past midnight, when we finally settled into slumber for the night. We arose early Monday morning feeling rested, refreshed and satisfied.


WE HITCHED DAISY to the wagon, then loaded about fifty pounds of our gold ore and covered it with canvas. We tied the mule to the rear on a leading rein and started out. The town was still asleep when we reached the post office, and we transferred the gold inside unobserved. Mandy went on to the livery stable to leave Daisy for the day and deliver our "rescued" mule to its temporary home while it waited to be claimed by its rightful owner. I moved the gold in small batches to the rear of the building, where it would be assayed, tagged, and deposited in the bank for safekeeping.

As I reviewed the procedure in my mind, it struck me that Mandy, and only Mandy, had knowledge of all communication both into and out of Weaver's Flat. Every piece of incoming and outgoing mail passed through her hands. She personally handled every incoming and outgoing telegraph message. She acted as Receiving Agent for every stagecoach shipment and completed the manifests for outgoing shipments.

I realized that Mandy had the ability, if she ever chose to use it, to control the town simply by manipulating its communication with the outside world. She could also, if she wanted to, run any kind of clandestine operation involving transfer of materials and consequent accumulation of wealth in a distant place. I looked at our pile of gold ore. More pieces of the puzzle that was Amanda Wells began to fall into place.

"What's going to happen to this gold?" I asked when she came in a few minutes later.

"It gets assayed and sent to be refined." She shrugged. "Is that what you're asking me? You already know how it works."

"I want to know more. When you assay it, what exactly do you do?" I asked her.

"Well, long story short, I figure out the total weight and what percentage of it is gold. It can get a little tricky, but there's no great mystery once you get the hang of it."

She didn't seem to be evading me, but she wasn't telling me what I wanted to know, either. I had a sudden fear that she was withholding something. I feared her feelings for me might be a charade, that she was keeping me around only because I had discovered too much, and that she planned to leave me behind with Seth when she fled Weaver's Flat. I couldn't bear the thought. I needed to have everything out in the open, and I was determined to make it happen.

"I want to know how this pile of rocks gets turned into money. And where that money is. And if you really do love me as you say you do. And what your intentions are for our future together."

She laughed. She actually threw back her head and laughed and said, "Oh, dear Lord!"

"Well?" I demanded.

"I'll answer your questions in order. The ore goes to a refinery. The refinery extracts the gold and sells it to the U.S. Treasury. They take out their cut from what the Treasury pays them and issue a draft for the balance to the person who gave them the ore in the first place. And that person does whatever they want with the draft—probably puts it in a bank."

She stepped closer and took me in her arms. "Now as to your other questions: I really do love you, more than words can say, and I plan to spend the rest of my life with you." She stepped back and held my hands in hers. "And yes, that really was the Lost Dutchman Mine, and no, I've never shown it to anyone else, and no, I'm still not telling you everything, because you'll have to see it for yourself when we get to Phoenix."

It took my breath away. I started to sputter a response when Martha Mae burst through the front door.

"I thought you might like to know how your fiancé is doing," she said to me.

"He is not my fiancé. His condition does not concern me, except to the extent that he might be able to harm Mandy and me."

She smirked at Mandy and continued. "I don't think he'll be harming anyone for quite some time. After Mandy dropped him off, he had a little...mishap."

"What sort of mishap?" Mandy asked.

She smiled sweetly. "It really was an accident. Honestly. When Caleb and Hank were helping him up to his room, he started to regain consciousness and jerked a little. And they sort of...dropped him."

"On the stairs?"

"Sadly, yes. Almost at the top step." She grinned. "He fell all the way down and broke his leg."

Mandy nodded. "I see."

"So they carried him back up and deposited him in his room. They gave him a bottle of whiskey to ease the pain. Of course," she said mischievously, "water is of no use as a painkiller. So they didn't bother with that."

"Are you saying that he has no water to drink? Just whiskey?" I asked.

"For medicinal purposes only," Martha Mae said with a little nod. "He's confined to his room until Doc Hudson gets here to treat that leg—and the broken jaw of course—so he needs plenty of whiskey for the pain."

Mandy said, "I almost feel sorry for the miserable bastard."

"Oh, you needn't." Martha Mae shook her head. "The girls are giving him the best of care. We bring him all his food and empty his chamber pot. We take the notes he writes and...well, we provide written responses that we believe will please him, with the signatures he hopes to see."

"You mean, you're forging letters to him?" Mandy asked.

"The girls think of it more as providing comfort to a very distraught patient." She replaced her hat and picked up her handbag. "I have to get back now." She glanced at me. "I knew you'd want to know about your fiancé's condition, so I made time to squeeze in this little visit. Keep up the good work," she said over her shoulder as she went out.

I looked at Mandy in disbelief. Whether Seth knew it or not, he was a prisoner at Emery's. He was trapped upstairs with a broken leg, unable to speak through a broken jaw, unable to get written communication past the women at Emery's to the outside world. And with nothing to drink but whiskey, he was undoubtedly incoherent most of the time.

"That was nice of Martha Mae," said Mandy.

"Nice?"

"She bought us some time. Just now she gave us an idea of how much time."

"Time for what?"

She frowned. "Basically to pull up stakes and disappear from Weaver's Flat. I'd say we have a little more than two weeks. That should be enough to ship out all the gold ore, fabricate a story about why I have to leave, and move my possessions to Phoenix."

I was overcome with sadness and guilt. Because of Seth and me, Mandy's life was ruined. She would leave Weaver's Flat in order to draw Seth away before he could tell the men what he already knew, and before they learned the true nature of the charity circle and other secrets that would destroy so many more lives.

I began to cry. "This is all my fault. I used to think I was so clever, playing you for a fool, deceiving you as I did on Seth's behalf. Now I've ruined everything."

"That isn't true, April." She gripped my shoulders and looked at me intently. "You haven't ruined anything. This was my plan from the beginning. I just didn't intend to leave so soon. I was going to stay for three more years. But I'm leaving now. That's all." She shook my shoulders gently. "You haven't ruined anything. Besides, you've made me happier than I've ever been in my life."

MANDY SPENT MOST of the morning assaying the gold and packaging it for transport. But when closing time drew near, she didn't load it onto the cart to take to the bank, as she had in the past. Instead she pulled the wood stove into the middle of the room and pried up several floorboards.

Under the floor, enough soil had been removed to form an opening about six feet long, two feet wide, and two feet deep. The opening held a metal casket. The sight of it shocked me.

"Is somebody buried in there?" I asked.

She smiled. "No, it's nothing as sinister as that. When I'm dealing with my own gold, I don't take it to the bank for safekeeping." She glanced out the window in the direction of the bank. "There are a lot of curious eyes and ears over there. Large amounts of gold ore, like what we'll be handling, raise too many questions. The fewer people who know about this, the better it will be."

"But...a casket?"

"Think of it as just a metal box," she said with a laugh. "Wood tends to rot. This won't. And it's just the right size."

I helped her lower the packages of ore into the casket. Then she replaced the floorboards and pushed the stove back to its original position.

"What about the stagecoach driver? He must wonder about huge shipments like this, and where they're coming from," I said.

"Amos? No, he's used to it. Dozens of people ship ore out of here on the stagecoach. It adds up to quite a bit. The shipping labels are all the same: from Weaver's Flat Assay Office to Williamson Refinery in San Francisco. That's all Amos knows."


THE NEXT DAY we brought in seventy pounds of ore on the wagon. Mandy had it assayed and packaged by late morning. Since it was Tuesday and the stage was due in the afternoon, we stacked the packages in the post office lobby. Then we retrieved the ones from yesterday's effort and added them to the pile. Mandy checked her gun and scanned the street outside. I wondered if Tuesdays had been problematic in the past.

The stage arrived on time. They exchanged outgoing and incoming mail sacks, then Mandy and Amos wrestled the boxes of ore onto the rear cargo area and secured them. As usual, Amos was anxious to move on to Emery's, and the horses seemed just as eager for a shady stop at the livery stable. The entire transaction was over in less than fifteen minutes.


IN THE DAYS that followed, we repeated the routine. Every morning we brought in between sixty and eighty pounds of ore to be assayed. We stashed it in the casket under the floor, where it remained until Tuesday.

In all, the shipment weighed almost four hundred pounds. Amos grumbled about the weight. Mandy just shrugged and told him two old prospectors had hit a rich vein north of the Superstitions.

Although nobody knew it, the following week was to be our last in

Weaver's Flat. Mandy wouldn't tell me what she intended to do about Seth, but whatever it was, it never came to pass.


MARTHA MAE CAME into the post office on Friday morning. I couldn't read her expression. Her face was somber but her eyes were laughing. Momentarily I understood.

"Poor Seth," she said. "Poor, poor Seth."

"What's wrong with him?" Mandy asked.

"Well...basically he's...dead."

"Dead?" I cried. "What happened?"

"He got confused, I suppose. Fell out of his bedroom window. Or perhaps he jumped out...by mistake. Broke his neck." She examined the sleeve of her dress and said, "I don't know. Perhaps we should have given him some water. He drank a couple of gallons of whiskey last week...for his pain, you know. But no water." She examined the hem of her dress. "Water is no good for pain."

"I see," said Mandy.

"Do you still have his horse?" she asked.

Mandy nodded. "Yes. His name is Bingo. Gelding. Not a bad horse. Do you need it to cover burial expenses?"

"I think that would be a fair exchange." She poked around for something in her handbag.

"I'll bring the horse by tomorrow morning," Mandy said.

"Excellent. I have to get back to Emery's now. Keep up the good work," she said as she hurried out.

Mandy looked out the window. She watched Martha Mae make her way up the street to Emery's. "I have a feeling we're getting out of here just in time," she said.

"Why do you say that?" I asked.

She shook her head. "It's the mine. Too many people know about it. Seth had it just about all figured out. And the way he died—his mind must have been in a fog for almost a week. Who knows what he said, and who heard him?"

She spun around and walked to the telegraph machine in the back room. She frowned in concentration as she tapped out a message. After tapping for several minutes, she stopped and leaned back. A moment later, there was a brief series of taps in response.

"We'll need some help when we get to Phoenix," she told me. "I sent a message to...someone you'll meet."


WE LEFT THE following Wednesday. Mandy had notified Clyde Preston, who worked at the bank and was also the Mayor of Weaver's Flat, that she had been called away for a family emergency. The sudden terminal illness of her mother-in-law (who didn't actually exist) required her immediate presence in San Francisco.

The last of the gold ore had gone out on the stagecoach the day before. We left town with a few of our personal possessions, some food and little else. Pulling the light load on the wagon was an easy task for Daisy.

# Chapter Five

IT WAS MIDAFTERNOON when we arrived in Phoenix. We came to a stop in front of a small house on West Jackson Street, not far from the railroad station. A grizzled old man was slouched in a chair on the porch, apparently asleep.

When Daisy snorted, he looked up and smiled broadly. "Mandy, sweet fraulein!" he shouted. "I've been waiting for you."

She jumped off the wagon and ran to him. They hugged and rocked from side to side, as old friends often do when they haven't seen each other in a long time.

After a few moments, he looked up at me. "And who is this?" he asked. His German accent was heavy.

"This is April. She's very special to me," she told him. To me she said, "April, come and meet my friend Jakey."

I stepped off the wagon hesitantly. He enveloped me in a bear hug. "Very special, indeed," he said.

When I glanced up, I saw him wink at Mandy. She smiled and nodded almost imperceptibly.

"Is Julia home?" she asked.

"No. She's at the shop. She still insists on working long hours, although she doesn't have to. I've told her over and over. She doesn't have to."

Mandy said, "Jakey's...uh...friend Julia owns an ice cream parlor downtown. She works hard at it."

"Although she doesn't have to," said Jakey, shaking his head. "Come, let's go inside."

The house was spotlessly clean. The furniture was imported, mostly from England and France, all expertly crafted from fine wood and fabric. Jakey asked us to wait in the parlor while he went to the kitchen for refreshments. Momentarily he appeared carrying a tray with three steins of German ale and a large platter of cheese and crackers. We sat in Queen Anne chairs surrounding a mahogany table, where he placed the tray.

He took a gulp of ale, smiled with satisfaction, and turned to Mandy. "Now, tell me what you've done."

"I'm afraid I've made a mess of things, as far as the mine is concerned."

He cocked his head. "How so?"

"A few people somehow deduced that I know things about the mine." She shrugged. "Apparently there's been talk...questions about how I can afford to maintain the ranch on the salary I make."

"But you have the story about your dead husband. Don't they

believe that as a widow —"

"No, that's exactly where the story didn't hold up. April is the one who alerted me to it. The Fletcher boys carried the gossip all the way to St. Louis."

"Fletcher boys?" He raised his eyebrows. "Are they the ones whose parents died in the fire last year?"

"Yes. They live with their aunt and uncle now. They attend a school where April's fiancé was the athletic coach."

He looked at me. "You have a fiancé?"

"Not anymore. He's dead," I said lightly. Too lightly. But it was out and I couldn't take it back.

He turned to Mandy. "Did you..."

"Oh, no! I broke his jaw when he tried to molest April. But I didn't kill him."

"I see. How did he die, then?"

Mandy shrugged. "I think Martha Mae and a couple of the women from Emery's may have had something to do with it. There might have been some concern with maintaining secrecy about the charity circle activities. But there's no actual evidence."

He rubbed his chin. "Who else is suspicious about the mine?"

"Half the town," I said. "When I arrived in Weaver's Flat, before people realized my connection with Mandy, they weren't mindful that I overheard their gossip."

"We shipped out almost four hundred pounds of ore, Jakey," said Mandy. "Half of it's yours."

He shook his head and laughed. But I didn't laugh. I looked at Mandy and she must have read my expression.

"April, the mine...Jakey owns the mine."

"But that can't be! If the Lost Dutchman Mine belongs to anyone it's Jacob...."

"Jacob Waltz," he said as he dipped his head, "forever indebted to Mandy Wells, and happy to be of service."

I was stunned. I looked repeatedly back and forth between them. They gazed back at me expectantly, waiting for my reaction. I had no idea what to say.

"I...I'm...overwhelmed," I sputtered. "Of all the possibilities I imagined when we left Weaver's Flat, this one never occurred to me."

Jakey said, "Good. If you didn't figure it out, neither will anyone else."

Our conversation was interrupted by the sound of a door opening and closing at the rear of the house. We heard objects being dropped noisily and a female voice muttering annoyances. Then she appeared at the door of the parlor.

"Mandy, I'm glad you made it safely. I was so relieved to see Daisy outside," said the tall beautiful Negro woman. She nodded at me, smiled, and said, "I'm Julia Thomas."

"April Reynolds. I'm pleased to meet you, Miss Thomas."

She went to Jakey and kissed him lightly on the lips. "I have good news," she told him.

"You heard from the court?" he asked.

She nodded. "Since I used only my individual earnings to pay off the mortgage on the land, they awarded me sole title."

"That's wonderful news," Mandy said. "What happens next?"

Julia glanced at me and seemed to read my puzzled expression. "My husband deserted me over a year ago," she said. "He left me with a business — an ice cream parlor and bakery — and the land it sits on." She shrugged almost imperceptibly. "Unfortunately, he had used everything we owned as collateral on a series of loans."

"Obviously, he is not an honorable man," Jakey said.

Julia turned to Mandy. "The business is making a profit. Next, I plan to pay off the loans on the fixtures and equipment."

"You don't have to do that," Jakey said. "I wish you'd let me take care of those debts and be finished with it."

She sat on the edge of his chair and stroked his forearm. "I know I don't have to. But I want to. I want the business to be mine because I worked for it and earned it with my own labor."

He hung his head. "I wish you'd let me help," he grumbled.

She gave his arm a pat and jumped up abruptly. "Now, Mandy, you need to see to Daisy before supper. I'll start putting the meal together. Jakey, you and April have a little time to get acquainted."

Mandy went out to fetch Daisy and take her to Jakey's barn for the night. Julia went to the kitchen. Suddenly I found myself alone with the legendary Jacob Waltz.


HIS EYES TWINKLED as he looked at me. "I've never seen Mandy so taken with a lady...I mean...uh...with a friend before," he said.

The expression on his face combined with his tone of voice made me realize that he knew Mandy and I were lovers. And he was happy about it. I wasn't sure how to respond. Our conversation was interrupted by Julia, who brought in two more steins of dark ale. She placed one on the table in front of me. She stepped over to Jakey and kissed him on the forehead as she handed him the second one.

"You read my mind," he said.

"Your mind is an open book, sweet pea," she answered lightly.

Of all the terms of endearment she might have chosen for the crusty prospector, "sweet pea" seemed to me a most unlikely choice. When she looked at me and winked as she left the room, I couldn't suppress a smile.

"I'm curious about your fiancé," Jakey said. "Especially about how Martha Mae fits into the picture."

I wondered what information he wanted. Did he know that Martha

Mae derived sexual pleasure only from women? Did he know about the clandestine extracurricular activities of the charity circle? Surely he couldn't believe that Martha Mae would be upset by having sexual relations with Seth, or any other man. That was how she earned her living, after all. I decided to feign ignorance.

"Seth had a couple of serious injuries," I said. "Martha Mae was kind enough to try to nurse him back to health."

He raised his eyebrows. "Just how serious were these injuries?"

"There was his broken jaw, as Mandy already told you. I don't really know how serious that was, but his face was quite swollen and he couldn't speak. There was also an accident when he fell down the stairs at Emery's. That's when he broke his leg, and they put him in a bed upstairs. He wasn't able to move around at all."

Jakey rubbed his chin again, but not before I saw the hint of a smile. "I see. Trapped at Emery's and unable to speak. And then?"

"Nobody knows exactly how he died. His body was found on the street below his bedroom window." I shrugged. "Some people believe he must have tried to get out of bed and walk on that broken leg, and that he tripped."

"Yes, I can see how that could happen," he said, no longer concealing his amusement. "He got up and tripped out of the window and fell to his death. Of course."

"I know it sounds farfetched, but it's the only theory that anyone has put forth so far."

He took a big gulp of ale, then smiled with satisfaction. "There's more to every story than will ever be known. Martha Mae and I have a history, you might say, that goes back several years. I used to know her...quite well. I know how she operates, and how she survives. There will always be a special place in my heart for her."

It almost sounded like Jakey had in the past been physically intimate with Martha Mae. Her regular customers knew nothing of her taste for women. Had he been one of those men?

"Do you plan to stay in Phoenix?" he asked.

I breathed a sigh of relief that the subjects of Seth and Martha Mae were apparently closed. The disconcerting question of my entire future was next on the agenda.

"I have no idea what's to come," I said. "Mandy told me only a few weeks ago that we needed to get out of Weaver's Flat. But as to where we'll go from here, we haven't discussed it at all."

He gazed into space, deep in thought. "With your fiancé gone, I doubt that anybody in Weaver's Flat is aware of anything they're not supposed to know." He looked at me. "Even so, it would be better for you to go far enough away so that nobody from Arizona will cross paths with you — maybe California."

"California?" Mandy asked as she entered the parlor. "Why do you think we should go to California, Jakey?"

"You'll be safe there," he said. "From what I can ascertain, you've burned some bridges in Arizona."

"Perhaps. But to my knowledge, Seth Thompson is the only person who got close to putting all the pieces together. When he realized that April had shifted her loyalty from him to me, he began to express his suspicions about us. But that didn't continue for long, because he came to my place to take her away from me, and that's when I broke his jaw." She grinned. "He didn't say much after that."

"But he could have written out what he knew," Jakey said.

Mandy nodded, still grinning. "He could have, and he did. According to Martha Mae, he even documented his suspicions about the charity circle. But he didn't know that she was a part of it, and he asked her to deliver his notes and letters." She threw out her arms in mock horror. "And *poof*—they disappeared!"

"Then we don't have an urgent situation to deal with."

"I don't believe so. I wouldn't attempt to move back to Weaver's Flat, but I think it would be safe to make one more run to the mine...if you would accompany me, that is."

"You don't have to do that," he grumbled. "Haven't you read the bank statements I've mailed to you? You're already a wealthy woman."

I understood almost nothing of their exchange. Although I wouldn't press Mandy for information while Jakey and Julia were present, I resolved to ask her for the details that evening, when at last we were alone.

I didn't have long to wait. Julia served a light meal, and we excused ourselves early, pleading exhaustion from the trip. We carried two small valises to a lovely room that had been painted in pastel blue and furnished with a dressing table, writing desk and two comfortable chairs. There was one bed. Looking back on the evening's conversation, I realized that Jakey understood the nature of our relationship.


IT WAS ONLY a matter of minutes before we lay in the dark, under the covers in each other's arms. I was determined to find out about the mysterious references in the various conversations between Mandy and Jakey.

"I want you to tell me everything," I said. "So much doesn't make sense to me. I really need to understand what's going on, Mandy."

"I hardly know where to begin," she said with a sigh. "And it's too much to absorb all at once. But I'll tell you the important parts. You already know that Jakey is Jacob Waltz, that most people believe Jacob is the only white person who knows the whereabouts of the Lost Dutchman Mine, and that you have actually been inside of the so-called mine yourself."

"Yes, I do know that much," I said impatiently.

"And you know about the charity circle—that in addition to their volunteer work, the women often engage in sexual encounters with each other."

"Yes, I'm aware of that. And I'm aware that Seth may have deduced it as well," I said.

"Okay. And Jakey. Jakey, too."

"What does Jakey have to do with it?" I asked.

There was a long pause. And then, "Jakey is a woman."

"What?" I bolted upright in the bed. "What are you talking about? There are newspaper stories all over, property records, land claims. This makes no sense at all."

She pulled me down and wrapped her arms around me. "It's an elaborate fabrication that began way back when Jakey came to this country from Prussia in 1839." She proceeded to tell me enough of Jakey's story to give me an understanding of the present circumstances.

In 1836, Angela Waltz left her homeland to escape a future she dreaded. She didn't particularly dislike the man her family had arranged for her to marry. Although she had not yet discovered her attraction to women, she simply could not bear the idea of marrying *any* man.

Angela began to make her way across Europe, determined to reach the New World. During the journey, she realized that being female was a great disadvantage, so she disguised herself as a young boy and called herself Jacob. In Liverpool, Jacob got work as a seaman's apprentice on a ship that brought him across the Atlantic Ocean.

The status of women in New York was no better than in Europe. Matters such as owning property and having access to a bank account were relatively simple for a man, but could be problematic for an unmarried woman. So Angela disappeared forever, and Jacob set out to seek his fortune in America.

He worked an endless variety of odd jobs, always on the move, ever mindful that the discovery he was actually female would bring severe punishment. By the 1850s he reached Sacramento, where he mined the mother lode country to no avail for several years. He moved south.

Living in Los Angeles in 1861, he became a naturalized citizen of the United States. Then he moved to Arizona to continue his mining pursuits. He filed three claims in northern Arizona but finding no success, he moved on to the Superstition Mountains. It was there that Mandy and Martha Mae changed his life forever.

I realized that Mandy had reached a critical point in the story when she got up and lit the lamp on the bedside table. She picked up her dressing gown from the end of the bed and pulled it over her head. She sat on the edge of the bed and held my hand.

In 1881 a brawl took place at Emery's. There was nothing unusual about that. Gunshots were fired—again nothing unusual. Jakey, who happened to be in the bar, caught a stray bullet in his side. He bled profusely and eventually lost consciousness. Per the usual procedure, they carried him upstairs to an empty bedroom so that one of the women could patch him up if possible, hopefully avoiding a call to the doctor or worse, a call to the sheriff.

As it happened, all of the women were occupied with customers at the time, so Jakey was left alone and still unconscious in the empty bedroom. Some time later, he awoke to sounds of violence. He got up and made his way down the hall to where the noise was.

A woman was crying and pleading for mercy. A man was cursing at her. Someone was getting hit repeatedly, and very hard. Jakey opened the door. The man inside, furious at the unwanted interruption, spun and lunged at his throat. Jakey fell to the floor and his wound reopened. Then he heard a gunshot and the grip on his throat loosened. Just before he lost consciousness again, he saw the face of an angel kneeling over him, telling him that he had saved her life.

"The angel was Martha Mae, as you've probably surmised," Mandy said. "Martha Mae's customer had claimed he wanted her services, but what he really intended to do was rob her and kill her."

I nodded. "Jakey told me this evening that there would always be a special place in his heart for Martha Mae."

"That's certainly true, but it isn't because he saved her life. It's a bit more complicated than that. Jakey didn't regain consciousness again for a couple of days. Martha Mae did everything in her power to save him. In the course of her ministrations, she removed his clothes and discovered the secret."

"And she kept the secret, obviously," I said.

"She told me about it because she needed help to care for Jakey. I had been living in Weaver's Flat for less than a year at the time. They had just gotten the telegraph line, and I got a job there because they needed someone who knew Morse Code." She smiled and shook her head. "I went there with almost nothing. I lived on one of the ranches outside of town, in a spare room. The rancher's wife introduced me to the charity circle, and that's where I met Martha Mae. She and I were...intimate...for a while. Now we're the best of friends."

"When Jakey got shot at Emery's, you and Martha Mae were lovers?" I asked.

"That's correct. Between the two of us, we nursed him back to health and managed to keep his secret." She smiled. "We did it out of loyalty to...I don't know...our own kind, you might say. But Jakey is eternally grateful, and he's repaid both of us a thousand times over. I fabricated a story that my deceased husband's attorney had located me after several years of effort, and that I had inherited a sizable trust fund that enabled me to acquire my ranch. Through all the years, Jakey has continued to share his wealth with us. His generosity has never abated."

So that, to date, was the true story of the Lost Dutchman Mine. I knew for certain it was a story that would never be told.

# Chapter Six

WE STAYED AT the house on West Jackson Street much longer than we had anticipated. Every day, Julia took me with her to her shop. Mandy and Jakey, I realized, were at work on some elaborate plan, and they spent long hours in the parlor working it out. I knew I would learn the details soon enough.

Julia's shop was charming. On one side, behind the glass front of a long counter, were all sorts of interesting baked items. There were several tables on the other side of the room where patrons could sit while they enjoyed the coffee and ice cream she also served. It was a popular gathering place. Local residents brought newspapers and magazines, and there were always lively conversations about current controversies. Out of sight in the rear was an array of refrigeration and commercial baking equipment that was quite beyond my ability to comprehend.

Within a few days, I learned enough about the shop to operate it by myself for brief periods. This enabled Julia to take care of whatever errands were needed before closing time, so her workday was shortened by at least an hour.

During the slow period every afternoon, we had time to get better acquainted. After some initial verbal sparring, when each of us ascertained just how much the other knew, we happily exchanged the unabridged versions of our stories.

Julia had been married to a financially irresponsible white man, who was also physically abusive. When Jakey rescued her, she believed he was a man. Later, as their relationship deepened, she was overjoyed to learn the truth. Julia, Mandy, Martha Mae, and now myself were the only ones who knew. To avoid inadvertently revealing the secret, we always referred to Jakey as "he" or "him" or whatever masculine term was called for, even in private conversation.

Of course Julia knew that Mandy and I were lovers. She was fascinated by the story of how we met and that I had no idea of my true inclinations before Mandy entered my life. The irony of our situation — that we were four women who loved women, living as accepted couples under the noses of a totally intolerant but totally unsuspecting society — did not escape us.

As we finished supper one evening, Mandy cleared her throat in a manner that told us she had something important to say. All eyes turned to her.

"Jakey and I have worked out a plan," she began. "We don't know exactly how long it will be safe for me to stay in Phoenix. Under the circumstances, it won't be long until someone figures out what really happened to Seth Thompson." She glanced at me and then returned to scanning the three of us as she spoke. "Martha Mae hopes to stay in Weaver's Flat for about five more years. She's already a very wealthy woman, but her ambition is to accumulate more. We respect that. So if the question ever comes up, I'm the one responsible for Seth's death."

I began to protest. "But you didn't — "

"Because," she interrupted, "Martha Mae will still be in Weaver's Flat and she'll need a cover. Whereas I will be long gone to parts unknown."

"But not until we bring down one more load from the mine," Jakey added.

She shrugged. "We aren't in complete agreement on this point. Considering my bank account in San Francisco, I believe that April and I have enough money to live indefinitely in whatever manner we choose. Jakey believes we should start out with more."

"So we'll go up there tomorrow," Jakey said with a grin. "Julia and I have two horses and a mule. With Daisy, that makes four animals." He rubbed his hands together. "We can bring back quite a haul."

"Once we're out of Arizona," Mandy continued, "Jakey will plant a bug in a few well chosen ears about how I was the one who killed Seth." She looked at me and winked. "Jealousy," she said, grinning.

It struck me that these people were all quite mad. But perhaps it was simply the difference in our backgrounds. I was raised in St. Louis, a bastion of proper civilized society. They were frontier people who of necessity were concerned mainly with survival. And they were good at it. I vowed to work harder at adapting to their ways.


THE NEXT MORNING three of us set out for the Superstition Mountains. Julia stayed behind to work at her shop. Daisy pulled the wagon and I drove. The mule was tethered to the rear. Mandy and Jakey rode the other two horses.

When we reached the base of the Superstitions, we would have to leave the wagon and proceed single file the rest of the way. On the return trip, two horses would pull the wagon, which would be loaded with gold ore.

We stopped to rest and water the horses at mid morning, and again at around two o'clock in the afternoon. Mandy estimated that we were about four miles from the base of the mountains.

Just as we started out on the final portion of the wagon trail, I heard a strange sound. It started as a low rumble, and I couldn't identify its origin. It seemed to surround us.

Daisy reared back and tried to turn. I glimpsed the panic in her eyes just before she bolted off the trail. I pulled hard on her reins, but it had no effect. Suddenly Mandy came from behind on my left, riding fast. She grabbed the reins just behind Daisy's neck and brought her to a jerky stop, shouting out assurances to the panic-stricken horse. She dismounted and stroked Daisy's neck, trying in vain to calm her.

The rumbling grew louder. Hundreds of birds flew over us, all heading west, away from the mountains. All of the animals were terrified. I jumped off the wagon and understood why. The earth itself was trembling. We looked toward the Superstitions. Even from a few miles away, we could see that huge rocks which had perched atop the mountains for hundreds of years were falling like a child's wooden toy blocks. Dark clouds rose from behind the mountains. It looked like a volcanic eruption.

The shaking finally stopped, but the noise and destruction continued. Jakey joined us on foot, drawing his trembling horse behind him. We watched for several minutes as the Superstition Mountains groaned, roared, and violently rearranged themselves. Whenever it seemed that the worst was over, there were more loud cracks, almost like a thunderstorm, followed by more billows of dark red and black clouds.

"I'll be damned," Jakey finally said. "When I lived in California, I used to wonder if I'd ever be in an earthquake. But they're not supposed to happen here in Arizona."

Mandy said, "This changes everything. I don't think we'll be going in there for some time." She paused and squinted at the mountain tops. "Perhaps never."

"Perhaps never," Jakey whispered.


WE DECIDED TO return to Phoenix immediately, although we wouldn't reach the city until after dark. Traveling at night was somewhat dangerous, but the alternative was to camp where we were, and with the desert environment in a state of upheaval after the earthquake, the prospect was a bit daunting, even to Jakey and Mandy.

The lights of Phoenix came into view at about nine o'clock, and less than an hour later we were safely inside Jakey's house. Julia was overjoyed at our return. The earthquake had been felt strongly in the city, and she knew that if we had been near the mine when it hit, our chances of survival would have been slim.

We celebrated our safe return with Julia's fabulous coffee and generous servings of her special rum cake. That made Jakey think of rum, and soon the coffee was set aside. After our frightening experience, we felt fortunate to be alive. We drank and laughed and finally went to bed, exhausted.


MANDY WAS CORRECT about the earthquake changing everything. We spent most of the next week trying to get our bearings so that we could move on. Julia suggested that I come to work with her for a few days. She felt that the familiar routine of her shop would be comfortable for me, and it would give me something productive to do. I agreed.

At Julia's shop, as in the rest of the city, almost every conversation was about some aspect of the earthquake. Customers brought in newspapers from all over the Territory, and I learned many facts and details about what had happened.

One man brought in the latest edition of a Prescott newspaper, the Arizona Journal-Miner, which reported that the quake had been felt in El Paso, Deming, Tucson, Yuma, Phoenix and McDowell. The exact time had been determined to be 2:35 PM on May 3, 1877. The Arizona Daily Gazette reported that just after the shock, a dense cloud of dust hung over the Superstition Mountains.

We learned that soldiers from Fort McDowell, a few miles north of the Superstitions, rode into the area as far as they could. They reported that one side of the mountain range had completely broken down and fragments were scattered for miles in every direction, as though hundreds of tons of dynamite had exploded from beneath the base of the mountain.

Numerous huge fires on the hillsides were set off when rocks and boulders crashed to the ground. They landed with such force that sparks flew from them, igniting the surrounding dry grasses. The fires burned on and on, unchecked, destroying grazing land for miles around.

Ten days later, we could still see large dark clouds of smoke to the east and south. Mandy and Jakey decided to ride up to the mine, and then return by way of Weaver's Flat. They didn't plan to bring back any gold ore, but they wanted to find out if the mine was still accessible. On the way back, they would check on their friends in town. I was not invited to join them. After the trauma of the preceding days, I was barely holding myself together, and Mandy knew it.

ON TUESDAY MORNING, exactly two weeks after the earthquake, Mandy and Jakey set out on horseback for the mountains. As Julia and I watched them ride out, I realized that for the next few nights I would be alone in bed for the first time in months. I felt an emptiness in the pit of my stomach. The thought of not sleeping with Mandy, not feeling the warmth and security of her body wrapped around mine, was disconcerting.

It struck me for the first time that our relationship had flourished because of the intimacy we shared at night. It wasn't only our lovemaking — although that was undeniably a large part of it — but the emotional giving that seemed to spill so naturally from both of us as we exchanged our innermost hopes and dreams in the darkness of night. I had never been so happy as I was with this wonderful woman.

Julia tapped me on the shoulder. "They're out of sight, April. You can come back in the house now," she said with a smile.

I followed her into the house. Her shop wasn't due to open for an hour, so we made a small pot of coffee and sat at the kitchen table.

"I hope everyone in Weaver's Flat is all right," I said.

The road into the town was blocked in two narrow places by large boulders that had fallen from their perches above, so the stagecoach had not been able to get through, and the telegraph lines were down. Nobody had heard anything about the fate of the town.

Julia said, "We'll know in a few days. Jakey and Mandy won't come back until they find out if those people need help."

"Do you believe they'll be able to reach the mine?" I asked her.

She shook her head. "From what I've heard, it's pretty bad up there. I'd be surprised if they could ever find the mine." She took a sip of coffee and frowned. "Most of the landmarks were probably destroyed, and my guess is the ones that weren't got moved several hundred yards, maybe even a few miles."

Since the earthquake, every day at the shop had brought more bad news. As it turned out, this day was no exception.

One of Julia's regular customers was a man named Doc Hensley, a retired dentist from Chicago who had moved to Phoenix in hopes of curing his chronic bronchial problems. He avidly absorbed each story in every newspaper that was brought to the shop. He reported in great detail to the other customers, many of whom were unable to read.

Doc scrutinized the latest copy of the Arizona Weekly Enterprise from the small town of Florence on the southeastern edge of the Superstitions. "Now, this story can't be right," he began. "It names over a dozen rivers and lakes that supposedly aren't there anymore. It says they just caved in and disappeared. There's no more water."

There was much grumbling, and general agreement that the story was too far fetched to be anywhere near the truth.

Doc continued. "They say the water swelled up other places. Where the San Pedro River was just a creek with barely any water, now it's a gushing riverbed."

"Do you believe it's the same water that disappeared from the other places?" someone asked.

"I don't know what to believe," Doc said. "It goes on to tell about artesian wells and ponds suddenly popping up all over the Territory."

"Them newspapers is outta control, if you ask me," one man said, "spinning a wild tale like that and expectin' reasonable men to believe it." Most of the others voiced their agreement.

Unfortunately, they were to be proven wrong. Months later, when truth was finally separated from the many fanciful tales, a horrifying picture emerged. Blazing fires burned for weeks, destroying most of the grazing lands. Late summer rains washed away the topsoil, taking the grass roots with them. It would take years to re-establish the cattle industry in the Territory of Arizona.

THREE DAYS AFTER they left, Mandy and Jakey returned. They were not alone. Martha Mae Kellogg rode with Jakey on his big gelding. Mandy rode on Daisy, and behind them on a long tether was a very noisy mule carrying several bulging saddlebags.

The sight of Mandy thrilled me. I wanted to hold her and cover her with kisses, but because we were outside where someone might see us, I was forced to restrain myself until the animals were tended to and we were all in the house.

Then I threw myself at her with wild abandon. Jakey, Julia and Martha Mae whooped and cheered at my antics. Mandy scooped me up, blushing and laughing and kissing my face all at once.

When we finally settled down, Jakey filled five steins with dark ale. We drank a toast to life—specifically the fact that the five of us were still alive—then sat down at the kitchen table to work out what to do next.

"How did Weaver's Flat fare in the earthquake?" I asked.

"The ranch is completely gone," Mandy said. "The house collapsed. Most of the bricks broke in several places. It's the same with all of the adobe buildings in the area."

Martha Mae said, "Emery's was damaged beyond repair. The second floor collapsed onto the first, and the west wall buckled completely." She gave a little laugh. "It won't be 'business as usual' there anymore."

"What about the other girls? Were any of them hurt?" I asked her.

"No, we all escaped unscathed. Due to the time of day, we were all downstairs when the quake struck," she said brightly. "When the bottles behind the bar started to rattle and fall off the shelves, everyone ran out into the street. The building collapsed a few seconds afterward."

"Where are the other girls now?" Julia asked.

"They're in Tucson, if all went according to plan. Hank Edwards knows an opportunity when he sees one. He recruited the girls, or they recruited him, depending on your point of view. They took four wagons, ten horses and everything they could scavenge from Emery's to set up shop down there."

Julia cocked her head. "Why didn't you go with them?"

"Because I knew that Jakey and Mandy would come for me." She grinned. "I didn't want them to worry when they got there and I was nowhere to be found."

Mandy leaned over and looked into her eyes. "The truth, Martha Mae."

"Well...all right. I had a strong feeling when you and April left that you were going to California. I wanted to go with you—maybe live in a real city like San Francisco." She looked at Jakey. "And of course I knew that you and Mandy would come to my rescue as soon as you could after the earthquake," she added with a smile. "And with the mine gone..."

The mine! In all my anxiety about the fate of Weaver's Flat, I had forgotten about the mine. I looked at Jakey.

"It's gone," he said. "Or it might as well be. It's down there someplace, but nobody will ever be able to find it."

Mandy said, "It's buried under tons of rocks, and we couldn't tell exactly where to dig, even if we could move them. The boulders we used as guideposts got tossed around like pebbles."

So that was the secret fate of the so-called Lost Dutchman Mine. I knew that the legend would live on for many years. I also knew that the mine would never be found.

WE BROUGHT MARTHA Mae with us to Julia's shop the next morning. Although we were accustomed to her bawdy appearance and thought nothing of it, she caused quite a stir among the male customers. From his table stacked with piles of newspapers, Doc Hensley watched her with undisguised fascination, and she seemed to reciprocate his interest. She sashayed over to him.

"Mind if I join you?" she asked.

He stood, beaming, and pulled out the chair on his left. "I would be most honored, fine lady."

Doc's motive was clear, but Martha Mae had something else in mind. It soon became apparent, to me at least, that her interest was not in Doc himself, but in the information he might be able to provide.

Passing by their table during the course of serving the other customers, I heard fragments of their conversation: "...opportunities in the west...mineral hot springs...railroad goes right by...wealthy tourists...." It made absolutely no sense to me.

After about an hour, Martha Mae stood abruptly and said, "This discussion has been enlightening, Doc. I hope we meet again sometime."

He watched in surprise and obvious disappointment as she scurried behind the bakery counter and disappeared into the kitchen. As she went past, she glanced at me and signaled with her eyes that I should follow.

The instant I joined her, she said excitedly, "A golden opportunity is available to us!"

"What is it?" Martha Mae's idea of an opportunity wasn't precisely compatible with my own. But I was curious about her conversation with Doc.

"It's in California. Out in the desert. The railroad started running through there six years ago on the route to Los Angeles."

"A railroad track in the middle of the desert doesn't sound like an opportunity to me."

She shook her head impatiently. "There are towns being built out there. And there's water. They discovered dozens of hot springs. They're therapeutic, Doc says."

"Doc Hensley was a dentist, not a regular doctor," I reminded her.

She ignored me. "People with tuberculosis and things like that are brought from miles around to these mineral hot springs. And it works. They actually recover."

"I do remember reading something about that a few years ago," I said.

"It's starting to be a popular place. Last year a man named Doc Murray—and no, I don't know if he's a regular doctor—built a hotel there. It's called the Palm Springs Hotel and it has twenty-six rooms." She gripped my arm and looked at me intently. "Don't you see the possibilities, April? This is just the beginning."

"Perhaps," I said. "Let's talk it over tonight, when we're all together. There are so many details to consider."

"Oh, I have lots of details. It took Doc Hensley almost an hour to tell me everything he knows about the place, which is a great deal." She peeked around the corner at Doc, seated at his table reading a newspaper. "He's a very intelligent man."


THAT EVENING AT supper, Martha Mae related everything she had learned about the new desert community. It was located in a fertile valley called Coachella. For the past three years, water had been brought in via an elaborate aqueduct that had been built by an investor from San Francisco named McCallum. Agriculture was beginning to thrive. The Southern Pacific Railroad passed within six miles of the town of Palm Springs, attracting ever increasing numbers of visitors and permanent residents.

"So you see, the possibilities are endless," Martha Mae concluded.

"I can see endless possibilities for you," Jakey said with a laugh, "but what about Mandy and April?"

Mandy looked at me. "April, I think you must know by now that money isn't a concern for me. I have as much as I need, and I want to share it with you. I want to share the rest of my life with you."

I said nothing. All I could do was grin.

"I've thought long and hard about us going to San Francisco and retiring," she continued. "It would be safe. Or we could move to this place called Palm Springs and live with a lot of uncertainty about the future." She smiled slightly and raised her eyebrows. "It might turn out to be quite an adventure."

That settled the matter for me. "Palm Springs it is, then."

Everyone began speaking at once, congratulating one another and speculating about how to accomplish the move. We continued our happy babbling while we finished dessert and coffee.

Mandy and I made love that night with more intensity than usual. I realized that my cries of ecstasy, which I had previously managed to contain relatively well, were likely heard throughout the rest of the house. I was too happy to care.


PREPARATIONS FOR THE trip weren't nearly as complicated as I had anticipated. Since we would be riding on the train to Palm Springs, we left Mandy's wagon behind for Jakey and Julia.

Martha Mae insisted on taking the mule, and of course Daisy was coming along. The cattle cars, we learned, had separate compartments for domestic animals. We packed as much as the animals could comfortably carry in saddlebags so that once we arrived, we would be relatively free to move about in the Coachella Valley if the need arose. Everything else stayed behind.

We left Phoenix in the early evening. Once Daisy and the mule were safely aboard one of the cattle cars, we found seats in a passenger car near the front of the train. I dozed fitfully as the train rumbled steadily westward across mile after mile of desolate moonlit desert. Less than an hour after first light, I sensed a reduction in our speed, and we were notified that we were approaching Palm Springs.

# Chapter Seven
*Palm Springs, California, 1888*


WHEN WE STEPPED off the train, I was reminded once again of how far I had ventured from St. Louis. Rather than a busy depot bustling with activity, there were just two signs mounted on posts — one proclaiming that this was indeed the stop for Palm Springs and the other indicating that the town was six miles south (presumably along the deeply rutted trail that ran in that direction). Daisy and the mule were unloaded from one of the cattle cars and the train chugged away.

With the animals carrying our luggage, we set out on the six mile walk into town. While I suffered my usual anxiety over facing an unknown situation, Mandy and Martha Mae were obviously thrilled. Their pioneering spirit seemed to know no bounds.

We made it to the town before noon. We took two rooms at the Palm Springs Hotel, a two-story wood structure that had been completed just two years earlier and was already highly successful, thanks to the curative powers of the nearby natural hot springs.

Once we were alone in our room and I was safe in Mandy's arms, I allowed some of my distress to surface. I began to tremble.

Mandy said, "I realize how difficult this is for you. I'll do the best I can to make you happy here."

She kissed me, and even in my state of trepidation, I became more hopeful about our future together.


ALTHOUGH THE EXISTENCE and benefits of the hot springs were known years before, they were not accessible until the rail route from Los Angeles was completed. As an incentive to complete the job, the U.S. Government deeded title to the Southern Pacific Railroad Company of all the odd-numbered land parcels for ten miles on each side of the track in the area around Palm Springs. The trains began running in 1877.

By 1884, the area's first prominent white citizen had emerged. He was Judge John Guthrie McCallum, who came from San Francisco with his family in the hope that his tubercular son might benefit from the springs. McCallum bought land from Southern Pacific and built an elaborate aqueduct, bringing in enough water to establish a viable agricultural industry in the region, which by then had become known as Palm Valley. He was also instrumental in recruiting Dr. Welwood Murray to build the Palm Springs Hotel.

WE SURVEYED THE hotel lobby and the people milling about.

"There are opportunities here," Martha Mae whispered. She gazed at the staircase that led to the rooms on the second floor.

Mandy said, "You be careful, Martha Mae, until you find out how they operate in this town."

She smiled. "Of course. Let's find out about that this afternoon, shall we?"

After our midday meal in the hotel dining room, we took a stroll. Although the village was small, it was buzzing with activity. Over a dozen new buildings were in various stages of completion. The atmosphere was charged with excitement and optimism. The laborers were mostly Indians, and we learned that they were members of the Agua Caliente Band of Cahuilla Indians, whose ancestors had inhabited the area for hundreds of years.

Local law enforcement was entirely in the hands of Deputy Sheriff James Collier. We came upon his office just two blocks south of the hotel. Martha Mae said it was advisable to introduce ourselves so we would get off on the right foot in our new hometown.

James was a big, burly man with a hint of Scottish accent in his booming voice. He was probably in his late thirties, but his cherubic face and curly light brown hair gave him an almost boyish appearance. While he tried valiantly to include all of us in his explanation of his duties and responsibilities, he had trouble keeping his eyes off of Martha Mae.

The Sheriff's Office had the latest modern equipment. There was a telegraph machine. There was an impressive bank of rifles locked in a glass cabinet. To my surprise, there was a Remington typewriter — the first I had seen since coming to the West. Mandy was fascinated by it, and convinced James to show her how it worked. We left the sheriff's office knowing that we had found an ally.


DURING THE NEXT few months, each of us began to establish a comfortable pattern in our lives. I thought the deceptions we practiced were outrageous, but nobody seemed to notice.

Mandy ended up working at the Sheriff's Office. There was no money for a salary, so she told James the story of her widow's pension and struck a deal with him. In exchange for learning to use the typewriter, she did office chores and helped him to improve on his dreadful skill as a telegrapher. What she really wanted, unbeknownst to anyone in the area, was to be the first to know of any information that may emerge from Arizona concerning her prior activities.

Once she mastered the typewriter, she began to provide written accounts of local events to the nearest newspaper, the Herald of Banning, California. Her reports were clear and accurate, and they would remain so unless it became necessary to modify them for our benefit. She voiced frequent objections to James about the pittance the newspaper paid her for each story they published, but secretly she found it amusing.

For my part, I still had deep-rooted feelings of guilt and shame stemming from my role in the sham that Seth and I had planned to perpetrate against Mandy. To compensate at least partly for my evil deed, I sought out an opportunity to make a positive contribution to those around me. I found it with the Agua Caliente Indian children. While their parents worked tirelessly in the white man's world, lack of English language skills and understanding of cultural differences meant that they had no chance to improve their lot. But their children were a different matter entirely.

I had once heard that young children are able to learn a new language much more quickly than adults. Had I not witnessed it myself, I would not have believed it. I began with a half dozen children aged five to seven. We met for two hours each morning behind the hotel. To my amazement, in a short time their English skills approached those of white children their age. Their native language was quite beyond me, and their parents understood little of what I had to say. Nevertheless, the class was a huge success, and more and more Indians sent their children to learn the language and customs of the culture that was so strange to them.

I learned that in most so-called "Indian schools" run by whites, students were forbidden to speak in their native tongue or to practice their own customs. This was not the case in my class, as I found their ways to be enlightening and sometimes quite useful. The non-Indian population was less than pleased with my work, however, as they preferred to maintain a reliable, blindly obedient, low-paid labor force regardless of the consequences.

Predictably, Martha Mae set up shop in the Palm Springs Hotel. Some of the men were pleased with the arrangement (James Collier in particular), and the rest of them studiously ignored it. The women publicly pretended not to notice but disapproved vehemently among themselves.

When she wasn't working, Martha Mae visited a lady friend called Laura Workman, who was a clerk at the dry goods shop. Laura's husband John, an Australian immigrant, was one of the two gunsmiths in the town. He was the size of a grizzly bear and had a temperament to match. He alternately berated his wife mercilessly and neglected her completely.

Laura was a tall, slender blonde who failed miserably at her attempts to hide her beauty. She and Martha Mae became lovers within three months of our arrival. Mandy told me that Martha Mae had fallen hopelessly in love for the first time in her life. Fortunately, Laura felt the same. The townspeople thought it an odd friendship—a gunsmith's wife and a lady of the evening — but none of them had an inkling of the true nature of their relationship.


MORE AND MORE Indian children came to my informal class behind the hotel, until finally the manager informed me that my activity would have to cease. Although the children were well behaved, their increasing numbers were "annoying" to hotel patrons.

Mandy applied a bit of pressure to James Collier, who agreed (somewhat begrudgingly) to let me use the corral behind the Sheriff's Office. The children and the horses didn't seem to mind each other. In our makeshift classroom, I provided as much useful information as I could. But I felt that it wasn't always adequate.

I decided that firsthand experience would provide the best opportunity to learn about money and banking. The concept of finances and currency wasn't as mysterious to my young students as I had expected. They had learned at an early age the mechanics of bartering, the use of certain objects to represent wealth (as white men used coins), and the honor system of property ownership. But they were unclear about how a bankbook with a number in it was adequate to ensure that the bank would honor their deposits of white men's currency — especially if they didn't personally know the people working in the bank when they wanted to make a withdrawal.

Two of the children had accumulated over twenty cents in pennies and nickels. Each child could open an account at the bank, deposit his money, and receive a bankbook showing his balance. Their experience and future transactions would be shared with the class. They were enthusiastic about the plan.


I ACCOMPANIED THE two children who were to open accounts to the bank on a Tuesday afternoon in mid May. We took our place in line behind Emmy Burns, whose husband owned Burns Mercantile, and John Workman, whose wife was Martha Mae's lover. Never having been inside a bank, the children's eyes were huge as they stared in awe at every detail.

Suddenly the door slammed open with a loud bang. I glanced behind me. Two men, the bottoms of their faces covered by bandannas, stood with pistols drawn.

"Raise yer hands! Everybody raise yer hands!" the first man shouted.

He strode to the center of the room, his eyes and gun never leaving us. The second man went directly to old Jed Clancey at the teller's window and jammed the barrel of his gun under Jed's chin. He shoved a canvas bag across the counter.

"Put all the money in there," the man said. His voice sounded similar to that of the first man, but it was calmer, softer and lower. He glanced briefly at the customers, then back at Jed. "Make sure you get everything from the vault, if you care about these women and children," he growled.

I was both angry and frightened. I thought about the loaded derringer that Mandy insisted I carry in my handbag. Although I had never shot at a human being, she had taught me how to use the gun to defend myself if the need arose. I started to reach for the gun, then realized what a foolish thing I was about to do. It was better to let the thieves take the money than risk causing gunfire and endangering the lives of innocent people.

The first man, still pointing his gun at us, jerked his head toward my hand as I pulled it back from my handbag. In that instant, a shot rang out and he fell to the floor.

The other man screamed, "Curt, my God, Curt!" before turning to John Workman, who had just killed his partner.

John fired at the second man. Blood appeared on the man's shirt just below his shoulder and his gun fell from his hand.

His eyes blazed. "You'll pay for this," he screamed at John. "I swear, if it's the last thing I ever do, I'll make you pay."

Clutching his shoulder, he stumbled out the door. Moments later, we heard the sound of a horse galloping away.

Someone ran to the Sheriff's Office to fetch James Collier. Sensing an interesting story for the Banning Herald, Mandy came with him, her writing pad and pencil in hand.

James knelt down and pulled the bandanna from the face of the dead man. "Well, I'll be damned," he said. "I do believe this is Curt Franklin. Direct hit to the heart. He was probably dead before he hit the floor."

"Curt Franklin," Mandy repeated as she scribbled furiously on her pad. "Is that a name most people know?"

He looked up at her in surprise. "Most people? I'd say everybody around here."

Jed Clancey, who had gulped down several ounces of whiskey from the bottle he kept hidden behind his teller's cage, chimed in. "Yep, I recognized 'em the minute they came in, even with those bandannas over their faces."

"Them?" asked Mandy. "There were more? Where are the others?"

"Just one more," Jed told her. "Curt's older brother. Simon Franklin." Jed looked at John Workman and shook his head. "I surely wouldn't want to be in your boots right now. A man doesn't take it well when he sees his brother shot to death in cold blood."

James looked at the gunsmith and raised his eyebrows.

I said, "I assure you, Sheriff, it was self-defense. Those men were nervous and jumpy, and they were waving guns at us. John probably saved some lives by doing what he did."

Jed nodded in agreement. "Yep—women's and children's lives. Simon Franklin will come back for revenge, though. You can bet on that."

After James took statements from the adults who were present at the time of the holdup, the bank closed for the remainder for the day. My first responsibility, of course, was to my students. I wasn't at all certain how to calm their fear.

To my surprise, the children weren't the least bit frightened by the harrowing experience. They were curious. I assured them that the bank incident was not typical of the way white people do business. We planned to return the next day to complete our transactions.


THAT EVENING MARTHA Mae joined us for supper in the hotel dining room. She had already heard dozens of details, both true and untrue, about the earlier events at the bank. Although I was still shaken to the core, Mandy and Martha Mae saw nothing remarkable about the matter.

"Do you think Simon Franklin will be caught?" I asked.

Mandy said, "Probably not anytime soon. For one thing, very few people know what he looks like. His likeness has never been published in the newspaper."

"I wonder if Simon knows it was John Workman who killed his brother," said Martha Mae.

I thought back to the scene of the killing. "I don't believe so," I said. "He didn't indicate that he recognized John."

Martha Mae looked at Mandy and asked, "When do you suppose Simon will come back?"

Mandy said, "He'll wait until his shoulder is healed. Perhaps a month, perhaps longer." She took a sip of water. "Is Laura frightened for him?"

Martha Mae smiled sweetly. "I don't think 'frightened' would be the right word."

I said, "You don't mean she's hoping—"

"No, of course not," Martha Mae interrupted. "I only mean that she isn't frightened for John. He's big and strong. If anything, Simon Franklin should be the one who's frightened of another confrontation. John is a bully, and he enjoys hurting people. That's all I can really tell you about it." She grinned and shrugged almost imperceptibly.

Mandy laughed and turned her full attention to her meal. I wondered if I would ever understand the ways of frontier women. Her subsequent news story did little to enlighten me.

Curt Franklin Killed in Foiled Bank Robbery
Special Report to the Herald by Amanda Wells

Infamous outlaw Curt Franklin was shot to death

on Tuesday, May 15, as he and his brother attempted to rob the Palm Springs branch of the Bank of California. According to Sheriff James Collier, the quick thinking of bank patrons aborted the robbery attempt.

Among the patrons was Miss April Reynolds of St. Louis, who stated that the man later identified as Curt Franklin was in a state of extreme agitation and waved his gun wildly at everyone present. Fortunately, Mr. John Workman, a gunsmith who operates Palm Valley Hardware and Supply, was able to disable Franklin. "He probably saved the lives of some women and children," stated bank teller Jeb Clancey.

Simon Franklin, the dead man's accomplice and brother, escaped with a shoulder wound. His likeness can be found at the Palm Springs Sheriff's Office and in post offices throughout the region. Anyone who encounters him is advised to notify Sheriff James Collier of Palm Springs.

# Chapter Eight

IN THE WEEKS that followed, we moved from the Palm Springs Hotel into a little house that Mandy purchased near the edge of town. Like many of the homes in Palm Springs, it reminded me of Mandy's old ranch. Although we had moved over three hundred miles from Weaver's Flat, we were still in the Sonoran Desert, so the preferred building materials and construction methods were similar.

It was a cozy house. Fortunately, the previous owners had left most of their furniture. There was a huge overstuffed chair in the parlor, where I spent many hours reading, writing and planning. On the opposite side of the room was a magnificent mahogany table that Mandy was fond of using, as she had taken up writing editorials and "local color" pieces for the newspaper. Behind the house was a small stable and a corral for Daisy and her best friend, Martha Mae's mule.

I relocated my class for the Indian children from the corral behind the Sheriff's Office to our backyard. Martha Mae continued her activities at the hotel. In anticipation of the arrival of Simon Franklin, Sheriff Collier kept a watchful eye on the Palm Valley Hardware and Supply, and especially on John Workman. Our lives seemed to return to normal. Then trouble appeared where it was least expected.

BY THE FOLLOWING Sunday afternoon when Martha Mae came to supper at our new home, we had heard the details of her harrowing experience from every possible source, including the children in my class. Nevertheless, she launched into her own version of what had occurred.

"It happened late Tuesday night," she began. "It was unbearably hot inside the hotel, as it has been all summer. So as usual, we all sat on the front porch and chatted until past midnight. When I went up to my room, I encountered an unexpected visitor."

"Do you mean that you found a stranger in your room?" Mandy asked.

She smiled. "I thought he was there for the usual reason, so I wasn't alarmed. Only when I started to light the lamp did I realize that something was amiss."

"Why was he there?" I asked her.

She frowned. "He intended to harm me. I'm not certain why. He startled me when he knocked the matches from my hand. I jumped back, which I believe saved me from being struck a hard blow. His fist penetrated the wall behind me. He immediately began to curse and moan."

"And you didn't recognize his voice?" Mandy asked.

She shook her head. "At that point, I was focused only on escaping from the room. I located a water glass next to my bed, and smashed it against the table. I edged backward toward the door while I swung the water glass back and forth in front of me. Only once did the glass seem to meet slight resistance."

I glanced at Mandy. Rather than showing shock or dismay, she seemed to be absorbed by the details of the episode. Martha Mae, also completely calm, appeared to be working on the puzzle as she presented it. Apparently I was the only one who was shaken.

Martha Mae continued. "I reached the door, flung it open, and called for help. My cries drove the intruder away. He escaped out the window and fled. The sheriff and two hotel guests, all of whom happen to be familiar with my room, surveyed the damage." She shrugged. "Aside from the fist-sized hole in the wall and the broken water glass with a few drops of blood on it, everything appears normal. There were no clues as to the identity of the intruder."

Mandy asked, "Who do you think it was?"

"I've pondered that for hours," Martha Mae said. She shook her head slowly. "I don't recall anyone being unhappy with my...being upset with me for any reason."

"Supposing it isn't...related to business activities," Mandy said. "Have you had any problems in your...*real* life?"

Martha Mae grinned. "None at all. Laura and I couldn't be happier." She leaned over and whispered, as if there were imaginary people in the room who might hear. "John's mood is so foul these days that Laura avoids him as much as she can. That leaves more time for me!"

I said, "I would have expected the contrary, based on what I've heard about him. I assumed that he was happily anticipating a confrontation with Simon Franklin."

She frowned slightly. "Laura and I wondered about that too. He's barely mentioned Simon."

"He doesn't suspect anything about you and Laura, does he?" Mandy asked.

She knitted her eyebrows, obviously giving the matter deep consideration. Finally she said, "I can't imagine how he could know, but I suppose it's possible."

"I don't see any explanation that makes sense," I said.

Mandy stiffened slightly. "If there's no sensible explanation, that leaves all kinds of weird possibilities, especially in Martha Mae's...circumstance."

I thought about the many people with puritanical values whom I knew in St. Louis. Although attitudes were somewhat freer in the West, most of the rigid old ideas still prevailed regarding women like Martha Mae.

I said, "Perhaps the perpetrator objects to her profession. Or perhaps he just objects to the fact that she doesn't depend on any particular man for her livelihood."

Martha Mae laughed. "I know quite a few people like that. They have a lot to say about my morality during the day. But they're pretty quiet in my room at night. And I don't believe they're dangerous. Not physically, anyway."

Mandy said, "How about men who want to make believe they're somebody else? Could it be a man who wants to make believe he's...forcing you to submit?"

"Oh, Lord, Mandy," she said with a laugh. "Sometimes you surprise me by what you don't know. There are plenty of men like that. They have an arrangement with me." She leaned forward and spoke slowly, as if Mandy were a naïve child. "I am what they want me to be. That's my business. That's why I'm so successful in my business."

Mandy said, "Then the idea of actually forcing you—"

"Is a completely unnecessary waste of time, and they all know it," she said.

We tried in vain for over an hour to work out who had attacked Martha Mae. It seemed that we had eliminated all the possibilities.


LESS THAN A WEEK later, trouble erupted close to home. I hadn't thought much about the location of our little house relative to the Workman's, which was on the same road and barely a half mile farther from town. One evening about an hour after nightfall, there was a frantic pounding on our front door. Mandy hurried to open it.

Laura Workman, clearly shaken and trembling badly, burst inside and quickly slammed and locked the door. Her face was a mask of fear.

"What is it? What's wrong?" Mandy asked her.

She was breathing so rapidly that it took several seconds for her to say, "Someone just tried to kill me! He's still in the house!"

"What about John? Is he there too?" Mandy asked.

"No, he's still in town. Miles Cole is coming in from Banning tomorrow to pick up three of his rifles, and John hasn't finished the work on them yet."

Mandy went into the bedroom. She reappeared a moment later as she finished buckling her holster around her waist. I knew the pistol she carried was loaded. I was terrified. She grabbed her rifle by the barrel and held it out to Laura.

"You know how to use this, I assume," she said in a calm voice.

"Yes, but I don't think we should—"

"You'll be in danger every minute until the man behind this is stopped," Mandy said. Her tone left no room for further objection.

A full moon lit the road along the half mile walk to the Workman's house. As we approached, Laura noted that while she had left the house completely dark, lamps had been lit in the kitchen and parlor.

John Workman emerged from the house and ran toward us shouting "Thank the Lord," over and over.

Laura appeared confused. "John, I think there's someone here. I think he's hiding nearby."

"No, that isn't possible. I searched the property thoroughly after I didn't find you in the house. If anybody was here, he's gone now." He glanced at Mandy and me, then turned back to Laura. "What's going on?"

Laura told him about her encounter with the unseen intruder. He nodded and frowned, but I didn't see concern or fear in his eyes. Instead, he appeared excited, maybe even invigorated. His face looked as cold and cruel as I had ever seen it.

We walked home. The more I thought about the incident, the more puzzling it became. Was this a foiled burglary? If so, why did the intruder choose the Workman house, when there were other more affluent homes nearby? What did he want? Could it have been Simon Franklin seeking to kill Laura and even the score with John for killing a loved one? If that were the case, how would Simon have known that her husband wasn't at home?

"Things don't add up," I said to Mandy.

She nodded. "I know. We're missing some pieces of this puzzle."


WHEN WE GOT home, Mandy put the rifle in its rack next to the back door and returned her pistol to its place in the night stand next to our bed. Supposedly, everything was back to normal. But I was still shaken and I knew a sleepless night lay ahead. I collapsed into my overstuffed chair.

Mandy lit the lamp at her writing table. She intended to write a newspaper report of the evening's events. She stared at a blank piece of paper for several minutes, then looked up at me.

"What do you think happened tonight?" she asked.

I saw the problem. *Something* had happened, but we didn't know exactly what it was, nor why.

"We know that a man tried to kill Laura Workman," I said tentatively.

"Do we? She didn't tell us where she was at the time, or what the man did. She just said, 'Someone tried to kill me.'" She threw down her pencil. "We don't know why she believed that. We have no idea what really happened."

"We know that someone threw a terrible scare into her," I said. "The best actress in the world could not have appeared as Laura did, unless she was truly terrified."

Mandy stared into space. "I agree. What else do we know?"

I counted off on my fingers. "One: Laura's husband doesn't treat her well. But that isn't necessarily relevant. Maybe he simply doesn't know any other way to behave."

"I agree with that, as well," Mandy said.

"Two: Simon Franklin swore revenge against John Workman for killing his brother. He could seek 'an eye for an eye' and try to kill Laura."

Mandy nodded. "That's possible."

I continued on to shakier ground. "Three: Laura and Martha Mae are lovers. They don't think anybody besides us knows about them, but they might be wrong."

"That's also possible," Mandy said.

"Four: What happened tonight could be a coincidence. It's possible that a burglar picked the Workman house at random and Laura walked in on him. It may have no connection to the other events."

She grinned. "I'm not saying you're wrong. But I'm not a big believer in coincidence."

"Nor am I, but we need to allow for the possibility." I stood up. "In any event, I'm too tired at the moment to think clearly."

"Then the only thing to do is go to bed," she said with a wink.

But there was no romance that night. I lay awake, staring into the darkness. After about an hour I murmured, "Perhaps Martha Mae knows something."

Unaware that Mandy was awake, I jumped when she said, "Perhaps. I'll ask her tomorrow." She wrapped her arm around me and cupped my breast in her hand. "Go to sleep, sweet lady."

At last, I slept.


WE PAID A call on Martha Mae at the hotel the following afternoon. She had no inkling as to who had tried to kill Laura. But like us, she wondered about Simon Franklin's vow of revenge. If Simon's version of justice was to kill someone that John Workman cared for deeply, rather than to kill John himself, then Laura was still in danger.

Mandy stood and began to pace. "It wasn't Simon. It definitely wasn't Simon," she said.

"How can you be sure of that?" I asked.

"Because the Sheriff's Office got a wire from San Francisco this morning. Simon was found there and taken into custody."

"What did James have to say about that?" asked Martha Mae.

Mandy took a deep breath and said, "Nothing. He was out of the office when the wire came in, and I didn't tell him about it when he returned."

"But why wouldn't you tell him?" I asked.

"Think about it," she said. "Simon is the most likely suspect. But whoever actually tried to kill Laura is still nearby — perhaps waiting for another opportunity. As long as everyone is focusing on Simon, the real culprit is more likely to get careless and reveal his identity."

"I see your point," I said, "but I think you're probably breaking some law or other by not telling James what's happened."

Mandy nodded. "Yes."

WHEN I READ Mandy's newspaper report of the incident, I couldn't suppress my amusement. "You've perfected the fine art of using a great many words to convey no information at all."

She shrugged. "I can't report what I don't know."

Prowler Reported by Palm Springs Resident
Special Report to the Herald by Amanda Wells

Mrs. Laura Workman of Palm Springs reported the presence in her home on the evening of June 20 of a man whose identity was unknown to her. Mrs. Workman fled the premises and sought help from neighbors. Upon returning to the house, they encountered her husband, Mr. John Workman, who had apparently returned in the interim and frightened the intruder away. Anyone with information about the incident is requested to contact Sheriff James Collier.

# Chapter Nine

THE FOLLOWING WEEK was uneventful. There was no further suspicious activity at the home of John and Laura Workman, nor did anyone exhibit overly aggressive behavior toward Martha Mae. It seemed to me that life in Palm Springs had returned to normal. But my tranquillity was shattered quite suddenly one morning when Caleb McMann walked into the Palm Springs Sheriff's Office.

I was there in Mandy's absence. Since James Collier had become dependent on Mandy to deal with clerical matters and operate the typewriter, I took her place when she went to Banning twice each month on business related to her position as a reporter for the Herald. I still could not operate or even understand the telegraph machine. But if a message was sent to the Sheriff of Palm Springs that related in any way to Mandy or me, I would at least know of its existence.

The last time I had seen Caleb McMann was in Weaver's Flat. He and his wife Lurine had a ranch in the area, so I saw them occasionally when they came to town. I was relieved that Caleb didn't recognize me. Perhaps he didn't make a connection between the people in Weaver's Flat and those in Palm Springs. Or perhaps his mind was so completely obsessed with his mission that he didn't bother to look at me closely.

James had left several minutes earlier to respond to a call for assistance at the hotel, so Caleb had no choice but to address me directly. His discomfort was obvious.

"May I help you?" I asked.

"I'm trying to find my wife."

I knew that Lurline McCann was unhappy with her life, and especially with her husband. Mandy had told me about Lurline's association with the charity circle, so I also knew that she had probably been involved sexually with at least one woman from Weaver's Flat. Beyond that, I knew nothing about her, including her present whereabouts.

If I overreacted to his statement, he didn't seem to notice. I turned my face away in order to hide my surprise. In the next moments, as I attempted to compose myself, I fumbled for my pen and writing tablet. Then I took a deep breath and looked directly into Caleb's eyes.

"I'll prepare a report. We need your wife's name and physical description."

He answered quickly and accurately. I recorded his responses and continued.

"When and where did you last see your wife?"

He hesitated, apparently unsure of how to answer. He looked at the floor and shifted in his chair.

"Mr. McCann, did you hear my question?" I finally asked.

He looked up. "I sent her...I had to send her...away. To a hospital."

"Was she ill?" I was afraid I knew where this was leading.

"She was...confused. So I had her declared...I had her sent to a place where they would make her well."

"And what place was that, Mr. McCann?"

He buried his head in his hands. Over a series of fits and starts, the story emerged. Caleb had discovered Lurline's clandestine affair with one of Martha Mae's coworkers at Emery's Saloon. He had beaten her severely ("I'm her husband — it's my right..."), and eventually, with the cooperation of a local judge, had her committed to an institution for the criminally insane.

Three months later, Caleb wanted Lurline back. He went to the asylum where she had been sent and discovered that she was not there. Due to a series of inexplicable errors, she had been sent to the Yuma Territorial Prison, which held a handful of female inmates. For reasons unknown, she was released shortly after her arrival.

Just prior to her release, Lurline had told another inmate that she intended to go to Los Angeles to start a new life. But with no possessions and no money, it was unclear how she could complete the journey. She was last seen by the prison guard who unlocked the outside gate. He reported that she strode resolutely toward the railroad track.

The route was familiar to me. The westbound train ran through Albuquerque, Tucson and Phoenix, then on to Yuma, Palm Springs, and all the way to Los Angeles. Traveling on horseback, Caleb McCann was covering every mile of the route from Yuma to Los Angeles, in search of his wife. He assumed that she would be happy and grateful for the opportunity to return to him. He truly believed it.

Caleb intended to make inquiries around town about Lurline. To my knowledge, she had never come to Palm Springs, so his efforts would be in vain. However, if he came upon either Mandy or Martha Mae, it could lead to serious trouble. We had gone to considerable lengths to ensure that nobody in Palm Springs knew of our connections to Weaver's Flat, the famous Lost Dutchman Mine, the infamous Emery's Saloon, or the somewhat questionable events that had transpired while we lived in the area.

I didn't have much time to warn them that Caleb was in town and looking for information. Mandy was due to return from Banning on the stagecoach in two hours. Martha Mae was undoubtedly entertaining at the hotel at that very moment. I decided to find her first, then try to intercept Mandy on the road outside of town.

James returned from the call for assistance at the hotel shortly after Caleb left.

"I have to take care of a few chores," I said as casually as I could. "By the way, did you happen to see Martha Mae at the hotel?"

His cheeks turned pink. "How did you...uh, yes, I did happen to see her."

"Good. I'm heading in that direction, so I'll stop and see if she has time for a cup of tea."

I left the Sheriff's Office and hurried to the hotel as quickly as I could without drawing attention to myself.

Martha Mae was in the lobby chatting with one of the gentlemen who worked at the bank. When she saw my face, she excused herself and rushed over.

"April, what's wrong? You look like you've just seen a ghost."

"Worse than a ghost," I whispered. "Caleb McCann is in town. He's searching for Lurline all along the route from Yuma to Los Angeles." I didn't think there was time to relate the details. "It's a long story."

She put her hand to her chin and gazed at the ceiling. "Yes, I'm familiar with that situation." She looked at me. "Where is Mandy?"

"I believe she's on the stagecoach coming from Banning."

"That's good. If you can make sure she gets off the stage before it reaches town, Caleb won't see her. Meanwhile, I think I know how to cut his visit short. Tell Mandy to stay home and stay inside until she hears from me."

"But what about you?" I said. "This hotel will most certainly be one of his first stops."

She winked at me and said, "I'm counting on it. And I'm counting on you to keep Mandy out of sight for a day or two, so you'd best get moving."

I knew from past experience that Martha Mae could take care of herself. My warning about Caleb constituted the extent of what I could do to help. As she advised, I turned my attention to the problem of getting Mandy out of sight.

I hurried home. I shed my dress and pulled on a pair of Mandy's trousers and one of her shirts, then went to the stable. Daisy seemed to take on my own nervousness as I readied her to ride out to meet the stagecoach.

A FEW MILES out of town along the road to Banning, a large Mesquite tree offered shade from the blazing sun overhead. I dismounted, tied Daisy to the tree, and sat down to wait. Almost an hour passed before I heard the sound of approaching horses.

As if she knew my intention, Daisy moved back to the road the moment I climbed up on her back. When the stagecoach appeared, I took off my hat and waved it frantically. Mandy jumped out even before they had come to a halt.

"What is it? What's wrong?" she cried as she ran toward me.

"So far, nothing is wrong." I put on my hat and dismounted. "But there's a potential problem. Caleb McMann showed up in town today, searching for Lurline. He's going to be poking around in all sorts of places. So he's likely to discover that you're here, and he'll have a thing or two to report to the local citizenry, not to mention the Sheriff.

Mandy frowned. "Where is Martha Mae?"

"At the hotel. I warned her about Caleb. I have no idea how she plans to accomplish it, but she believes that she can compel him to leave shortly. Meanwhile, she says you should stay out of town, so that he doesn't see you."

She smiled almost imperceptibly. "I don't know what she plans to do, but I trust her. If you'll take my place here, I'll ride home on Daisy. I expect we'll hear from Martha Mae by tomorrow."

I boarded the stagecoach for the ride into Palm Springs. Behind me was a heartwarming sight that I never tired of: Mandy and Daisy going home at a slow pace, both horse and rider completely content with their world.


THERE WAS A crisp rap at our front door late the next morning. It was Martha Mae, with a mischievous grin on her face.

Mandy said, "Tell us what happened."

"Not until you bring me a cup of coffee," she said slyly. "I smell coffee. I want a cup."

Mandy heaved a sigh. I went to the kitchen and poured a cup of coffee. When I returned, Martha Mae was stretched out in my big overstuffed chair, ready to tell her tale. She accepted the coffee with a smile and began.

"As you predicted, April, Caleb's first stop was the hotel. I believe he intended to take a room there, and then explore the town and make inquiries." She took a sip of coffee. "But the first person he saw was me. I hugged him enthusiastically and our reunion progressed from there."

"Your fondness for Caleb is quite touching," Mandy said with a laugh.

"Yes, he thought so too. It was so touching, in fact, that he took me to dinner. After that, it seemed quite natural that he should walk me to my room." She smiled sweetly. "I felt obliged to invite him in for a drink and...well, the next thing I knew we were exchanging intimacies."

Mandy nodded. "Intimacies. Yes, I see."

"Oh, but you don't see," Martha Mae said. "We were physically intimate, which of course is of no consequence. I'm referring to the intimate information we exchanged about Lurline and her current whereabouts."

"How do you happen to know where she is?" Mandy asked.

"I'll get to that momentarily." She sipped her coffee. "The first thing you should know is that Caleb McCann is out of Palm Springs and on his way to San Francisco."

Mandy frowned. "Why did you tell him Lurline's whereabouts?"

"Come now, you know perfectly well that I would never reveal such a thing," Martha Mae said. "I merely led him to believe that it would be wise to look for...someone...in San Francisco. He left this morning."

I said, "Then she'll be safe in Los Angeles for now."

"Los Angeles?" Martha Mae raised her eyebrows. "Oh, you're referring to the tale she told at the prison in Yuma."

I nodded. "Yes, and the prison guard's statement that she headed directly for the railroad tracks when she was released."

Martha Mae laughed. "The guard spoke the truth. But it's not generally known what happened next."

"And that is?" Mandy asked.

"Lurline followed the tracks to the Yuma railroad station. Waiting for her there was Kitty Cole."

"She worked at Emery's Saloon," I said unnecessarily.

Martha Mae nodded. "And as you may recall, most of the girls from Emery's relocated to Tucson with Hank Edwards after the earthquake. They're doing exceedingly well there. Kitty, in particular, has cultivated a few very influential contacts."

"Influential enough to get Lurline transferred from the asylum to Yuma Prison and then released?" Mandy asked.

"Precisely!"

I was shocked. "Then Kitty must have blackmailed—"

"April, watch your language," Martha Mae said sternly.

Mandy said, "I assume that Lurline is in Tucson now."

"You are correct. When Kitty met Lurline in Yuma, they took the train east to Tucson, not west to Los Angeles."

"How do you know all this?" I asked.

"I received a letter from Kitty last month. They're both quite happy. Lurline learned how to operate the typesetting machine, and is employed by a newspaper called the *Tucson Citizen*."

I doubted that Caleb McCann would ever locate his wife.

# Chapter Ten

A FEW WEEKS after Caleb McCann's abrupt departure, I began to feel that we were safe in Palm Springs. I assumed the likelihood was slim that anyone else from Weaver's Flat would appear and cause us trouble. In that assumption, I was correct. The trouble came from within the town.

On the night it began, Laura Workman appeared at our door, severely shaken. I wondered if the unknown intruder had returned to her house, but I soon learned otherwise.

Mandy eased her into a chair at our kitchen table and turned to me. "Where's that bottle of whiskey?"

I retrieved the bottle from the back of the cupboard, poured a generous amount of whiskey into a large drinking glass, and placed it in front of Laura. Trembling badly, she used both hands to bring the glass to her lips. She swallowed, choked, grimaced, and returned the glass to the table.

"What happened?" I asked her.

"John somehow found out about Martha Mae and me. He knows about the two of you, as well. He's insane with rage. He's after Martha Mae, and both of you." She picked up the glass of whiskey and took a gulp. "He intends to kill you. If I expose him or reveal anything about my relationship with Martha Mae, he'll have me committed to an asylum."

I crumbled into the chair opposite Laura. "Does Martha Mae know?"

"Yes. I went to the hotel and warned her. Then I came directly here to alert you."

Mandy shook Laura's shoulders. "You need to pull yourself together," she said firmly. "Your life is in danger—all of our lives are in danger. None of us will survive without your help. Please, Laura. We need you."

Laura's eyes focused for the first time since her arrival. She looked at Mandy and said, "Yes."

As if she had suddenly awakened from a bad dream, Laura was no longer a traumatized, helpless woman. She was ready to do whatever was necessary to ensure our survival. I shuddered at the thought of what that might entail.

I bolted the doors. The moon was nearly full, so if John approached from the road in front of the house, we would see him through the front window. If he approached from the rear, the animals would smell him and hopefully sound an alert. Hopefully.

We worked out a plan to watch for John in alternating shifts.

Mandy fetched her rifle and handed it to Laura, who was positioned just out of sight near the front window. She retrieved her pistol, examined it briefly, and moved to the small window at the rear of the house. What followed was one of the longest nights of my life.

Ten hours later, when John still had not come after us, we assumed that Martha Mae was his first target. We feared for her safety. At the sound of a rapidly approaching horse, we moved cautiously to the front window. It was James Collier, and he was in a hurry.

Laura slipped into the bedroom, out of sight. James banged on the door and called for Mandy. He burst into the house the instant she opened it.

"There's been a murder," he said. "Behind the hotel. I have a hunch that the killer is headed for parts unknown, probably to the north. I need you to help me document the facts, and then wire them immediately to every law enforcement agency in the region."

My heart sank. I couldn't imagine the despair Laura must have been feeling. Losing the love of one's life was a tragedy. But hearing the news of her death while hiding in a strange room, together with anticipating the agony of having to grieve secretly, was unbearable.

Mandy looked at the floor. From where I stood, I could see the tears in her eyes.

I stepped forward and drew James's attention to me. "What happened?" I asked him.

"It's John Workman. He's dead. He's been murdered."

No sound came from the bedroom. I knew that Laura had heard the entire conversation. How she contained her emotions and maintained silence was beyond me.

James put on his hat. "I have to go up to the Workman house and notify Laura," he said grimly. He looked at Mandy. "After that, I'll meet you at the hotel."

"Don't bother," I said. "I'll take care of that. You have work to do, and the sooner you get started, the better your chance of catching the killer."

Visibly relieved, he made a hasty exit. As soon as he closed the door behind him, Mandy and I ran to the bedroom.

Laura sat frozen on the bed, staring into space. After a few moments, she turned to Mandy. "I don't understand what's happening to me," she said as tears began to roll down her cheeks. "When I thought Martha Mae was dead, I was in the pits of Hell. Then when I found out it was John who had been killed, I was actually happy." She shook her head. "I mean, I'm happy that Martha Mae is alive." She looked down and wrung her hands together. "I know that I should be devastated by my husband's death. But the truth of the matter is that I don't feel any sorrow at all." She covered her face with her hands as her tears flowed freely. "I feel so guilty. He was my husband, and I'm relieved that he's dead. What kind of horrible person am I?"

"You're not horrible at all," Mandy said. "You're a wonderful, honest woman." She knelt down in front of Laura. "Your feelings make perfect sense. Others might judge you, they might expect you to grieve for John. But that's of no concern. What matters is that you're honest with yourself about what you feel."

I handed Laura a handkerchief. She wiped her face and looked up at me. "Mandy is absolutely correct," I said.

I marveled at Laura's emotional strength. By the time we had walked to the Workman house, she was almost completely composed. Her thoughts had turned to Martha Mae's whereabouts and safety.

John's threat to kill us all was no longer a concern. Unaware of Simon Franklin's incarceration in San Francisco, most of the townspeople would assume that Simon was John's murderer. But I knew that there was a killer in Palm Springs whose identity and motives were unknown.

I STAYED WITH Laura until late afternoon. We discussed in vague terms what she might do in the coming weeks and months. There were decisions to be made.

She could sell John's gunsmith business, which made a respectable profit, or hire someone to run it for her. She could sell the house and buy a smaller one closer to town. She could continue to work at the dry goods shop, although financially it would not be necessary.

The most puzzling question involved Martha Mae. To Martha Mae's way of thinking, her profession was no different from most others. She had a particular skill, and she earned her living in the performance of it. She did not attach any particular moral, ethical, or emotional significance to her job.

Despite her best efforts, Laura had not reconciled herself entirely to Martha Mae's occupation. Nevertheless, she was determined that their love for one another would endure.

When I returned home, Mandy had already arrived. "Is Laura all right?" she asked.

"She's fine." I flung myself into my overstuffed chair and took a deep breath. "She's accepted what's happened, and she's considering the alternatives for her future."

"That's a bit more complicated than most people realize," Mandy said.

I nodded. "If you're referring to Martha Mae, I certainly see your point. With John gone, Laura doesn't know what to expect of their relationship."

"If memory serves," Mandy said with a grin, "she can expect a great deal."

"But Martha Mae will continue to live at the hotel, won't she?"

Mandy shook her head. "She'll continue to work at the hotel, and her work may keep her there overnight from time to time. But if she prefers to live elsewhere, she will."

"With Laura, for instance. Laura and I discussed the possibility of her buying a smaller house closer to town. At the time, I didn't connect that thought with Martha Mae."

She frowned. "I'm not sure the people here would take kindly to the two of them living together. Most of them already have a low opinion of Martha Mae. They would make it uncomfortable for Laura to carry on with her life once they found out that she and Martha Mae are...." She didn't complete her sentence, but instead gestured into the air at nothing.

The situation was far different from our own. On the surface, Mandy and I were accepted. We had arrived together in Palm Springs, and nobody had questioned the fact that we had stayed together.

Laura and Martha Mae were a different matter entirely. The townspeople would accept Laura, as a widow, taking up residence with another unattached woman. But not if Martha Mae was that woman. They would make Laura's life miserable once they learned of her new living arrangement. It was a difficult situation, and I couldn't think of a solution.

The more immediate concern, however, was the murder of John Workman. Known for his nasty temper and propensity for physical violence, he was liked by few and feared by many. Nevertheless, the list of people who might have killed him was short.

Mandy had spent most of the day at the Sheriff's Office helping James Collier prepare the necessary reports of the incident, and telegraphing information to concerned law enforcement agencies. She knew as much as anyone about the details.

"Does James have any suspects?" I asked her.

She grimaced. "He's sure it was Simon Franklin."

Of everyone in Palm Springs, only Mandy, Martha Mae, and I knew that Simon Franklin had been captured and was incarcerated in San Francisco. Much as he may have wanted to, he could not possibly have exacted revenge on John for killing his brother. "He's certainly the most logical suspect," I said. "But there can't possibly be any evidence against him."

"You and I know that. But an eye witness claims to have seen him behind the hotel just before John was killed."

"That's impossible." I leaned forward. "Who is this eye witness?"

"It's Martha Mae."

I wasn't certain why Martha Mae claimed to have seen Simon, although the report was certainly credible. Simon Franklin had publicly threatened to kill John. The yard in the rear of the hotel, where John had been shot to death, must have been almost completely dark at the time of the murder. It would be natural to envision the silhouette of the shooter as that of Simon.

"I think we need to have a serious talk with Martha Mae," I said.

Mandy glanced outside at the approaching darkness. "I agree. She's coming here for coffee and a chat tomorrow morning." She shrugged. "There's nothing more to be done for now. Come to bed with me, sweet lady."

I reacted as I had many times previously when our lives had been in the midst of upheaval. I needed Mandy in every way. She responded instantly when her simple goodnight kiss set me on fire. My body throbbed with a need that only Mandy could satisfy. It was much later when, fully sated, we fell asleep.

ALTHOUGH I ROSE at sunrise, I was barely dressed when there was a sharp knock at the front door. The instant I opened it, Laura burst in.

"April, I've been up for hours. I'm so worried about Martha Mae and—"

"Not to worry," I said. "Mandy saw her yesterday. She's fine. In fact, she's expected here shortly."

She followed me to the stove. "Is it all right if I stay until she arrives?"

"Of course it is." I prepared to boil water for a large pot of coffee.

Martha Mae arrived minutes later. Their reunion was tender and loving. Embarrassed by my intrusion on their intimate moments, I directed my full attention to making coffee. Then Mandy emerged from the bedroom, and the mood shifted subtly.

"I think we need to find out what's actually happened, and why it's happened," Mandy said.

I poured coffee for everyone. We gathered around the big writing table.

Mandy glared at Martha Mae. "You reported that you saw Simon Franklin in back of the hotel just before John was killed."

"Yes, that's what I reported."

"And the circumstances?" Mandy's voice reflected her impatience.

"It's quite simple, really. When April warned me of John's intentions, I decided that the safest place for me would be in the company of the Sheriff. So I asked James Collier to spend the evening with me. As usual, he was happy to oblige." She glanced at me. "I always provide free entertainment to officers of the law," she said by way of explanation.

Mandy said, "If you were with James all evening, how is it that you saw Simon Franklin and James didn't?"

"Easily explained," she said with a smile. "We had supper in the hotel dining room, then went upstairs to my room. During the course of entertaining James, we both fell asleep." She sipped her coffee. "We were awakened by the sound of a gunshot. I ran to my window, which as you know faces the rear, and I saw Simon running away. He was out of sight by the time James reached the window. But I assured James that there was no question of Simon's identity."

"And then?" Mandy asked.

"James pulled on his...James ran outside, but he was too late. By then Simon was long gone. But John's body was there, right where I had seen Simon a few minutes earlier."

Mandy said, "So that's why James didn't actually see Simon. His corroboration that Simon was there is based solely on what you said you saw from your window." She shook her head. "Martha Mae, you need to rethink this. It won't be long until people here learn that Simon Franklin is in jail in San Francisco, and that you could not possibly have seen him that night."

Laura raised her eyebrows, as if to question the incongruity, but Martha Mae's composure didn't slip even for a fraction of a second. "Maybe he escaped. How should I know? In any case, I see no reason to introduce more uncertainty into the issue at this time."

"No, I suppose that wouldn't help matters." Mandy sighed and stood up. "April, will you come with me to the Sheriff's Office? I have a great deal of work to do, and I'd certainly appreciate your help."

I couldn't suppress a smile. Mandy didn't need my help at all. But Laura and Martha Mae would be grateful for time alone together where nobody could find them.

"Let's go," I said.

> Palm Springs Resident Murdered
> Special Report to the Herald by Amanda Wells
>
> Mr. John Workman of Palm Springs was found dead behind the Palm Springs Hotel on the night of August 23. Hotel guests heard a gunshot just after 10PM, and one guest reported seeing the alleged assailant, wanted bank robber Simon Franklin, run from the scene. According to Palm Springs Sheriff James Collier, the victim died when a bullet fired at close range penetrated his right eye. Mr. Workman is survived by his loving wife, Laura. Anyone with knowledge of the incident is requested to contact Sheriff Collier.

# Chapter Eleven

THE SHERIFF'S OFFICE was empty when we arrived. Mandy went to her desk and I took the chair opposite her. She retrieved a blank sheet of paper and a pencil.

"What do we know about John's murder?" she asked.

I tried to put my thoughts into some semblance of order. "One: He was shot at close range. That could mean he knew the shooter."

"Quite possible," Mandy said.

"Two: His gun was found nearby."

She nodded. "James thinks he had drawn it with the intention of shooting his assailant. But he dropped it when he was hit. That's why it was on the ground and not in his holster."

"Three: Something prompted him to go to the rear of the hotel. But what could that have been?"

Mandy said, "If he went to the hotel with the intention of killing Martha Mae, as he had threatened, he wouldn't have gone through the lobby where people would see him. He would have tried to sneak in through the rear entrance."

"But he never made it inside," I said.

"Someone knew where he would be and intercepted him." She drew a rough map of the murder scene, including the rear of the hotel and the location where John's body had been found.

"Four: Martha Mae and James were awakened by the sound of the gunshot that killed John," I said.

She frowned. "I wonder about that."

"You wonder about what?"

"We know that John died from a gunshot. We also know that a gun was fired while Martha Mae and James were in her room at the hotel."

"You're saying that we can't actually assume—"

At that moment, James arrived. "Good morning, Mandy." He nodded at me. "April." He removed his hat and sat at his desk.

Apparently lost in thought, Mandy stood and wandered over to him. "Can I see your gun?"

"Sure. But what for?"

"I'm considering ordering a Colt like this for myself. I can get a good deal from a company in Chicago. I'd like to see if the balance and weight are right for me."

He handed her his gun. She turned away from both of us. I could hear the cylinder rotate, then the click as she snapped it back in place.

She handed the gun back to James. "It feels good. Do you fire it often?"

"Not much. This model should be cleaned after each use, and I don't like the work involved."

She turned to me. "April, will you join me for breakfast at the hotel?"

From the glimmer in her eyes, I knew she had something important to tell me. "I'd love to," I said.


"JAMES'S GUN HAS been fired recently. One of the chambers is empty, and I don't think he's aware of it," Mandy said.

We were alone in the hotel dining room. It was almost eleven o'clock, late for breakfast but too early for dinner. I sipped coffee while my favorite meal, scrambled eggs and toast, was being prepared.

"Do you think John Workman was killed with James's gun?" I asked.

"No. If that gun had been out of James's possession for any length of time, he would have checked it when he got it back. And he would have cleaned and reloaded it if it had been fired."

"But it was fired," I said. "And he didn't clean and reload it."

"Exactly." She leaned over the table and spoke almost in a whisper. "The gunshot that supposedly awakened James and Martha Mae...what if only James was asleep? What if Martha Mae fired his gun out the window, slipped it back into his holster, awakened him, and reported seeing Simon Franklin run away?"

"But John was killed at close range," I said.

"Yes. And I think he had been dead for some time when Martha Mae reported hearing the gunshot and seeing Simon Franklin."

Our meal arrived. We ate in silence. I pondered Mandy's theory. Even if true, it did not prove that Martha Mae had killed her lover's husband. In fact, watching Mandy deep in thought as she ate, I had a strong feeling that no proof would ever be found that Martha Mae had committed a crime of any kind.


I SPENT MOST of the afternoon with my young Indian students. They were learning to write in English. Since there were no school supplies, we made tablets by covering whatever flat surfaces we could find with wet sand. We wrote letters and numbers in the sand with styluses made from the thinner branches of the surrounding mesquite trees. So far, we had printed the capital letters of the alphabet, and then the words on some of the signs in town: BANK, HOTEL, DOCTOR, SHERIFF. From there, we would move on to the native names of the children, which had to be sounded out carefully to identify the corresponding letters in English.

My students were progressing rapidly. I realized that we would soon need pencils, paper, and reading material. I resolved to find a way to procure the needed items.


BY LATE AFTERNOON I was alone in the house. Martha Mae had gone back to the hotel. Laura had returned to her house to deal with matters related to her husband's death. I had just spread out in my overstuffed chair when Mandy got home. She had additional information about John Workman.

Dr. Bradley Henderson, the town's only practicing physician, also served as coroner. Mandy had accompanied James to Dr. Henderson's office to help gather the information needed for the sheriff's investigation and final report of the murder.

"John Workman's killer hasn't been identified, but an earlier mystery has been solved," Mandy said. "We have proof that it was John who attacked Martha Mae in her room."

"That proof being?" I asked.

"Doc Henderson found a bloody handkerchief in John's pocket. There was also a deep gash in his left cheek, although it wasn't obvious under his thick beard."

I said, "It's doubtful that he would have cut himself shaving. His beard was over an inch long."

"My thought exactly. But there was dried blood in his beard. That's how Doc Henderson came to notice the gash." She raised her eyebrows. "That reminded me of Martha Mae's water glass...the one she broke over her dresser and used to jab her attacker."

"I see that there's a connection, but that doesn't prove—"

"And, James had collected that glass as evidence. He retrieved it from his office. Doc looked at it under his microscope. Where the blood had dried on the glass, there were also two black hairs." She smiled broadly. "According to Doc, those hairs are from John Workman's beard."

Some of the pieces of the puzzle fell into place. John had somehow learned of his wife's affair with Martha Mae. Following his unsuccessful attempt to kill Martha Mae, he had become even angrier. He had gone home and terrorized Laura. She had escaped and taken shelter at our house.


THE SHOCK OF John Workman's murder began to fade. Palm Valley Hardware and Supply remained closed while Laura tried to determine whether to sell the business that she and John had built, or to reopen it with hired help. All other businesses returned to normal.

As she did every Wednesday evening, Mandy brought home the weekly edition of the Banning Herald. The newspaper had become the primary source of reading material for my students. Not fond of being taken by surprise in class, I began my usual task of reading the entire paper from front to back before passing it on to the children. I didn't finish.

I was brought up short by a brief article on page three. Notorious bank robber Simon Franklin was scheduled to appear in court in connection with a robbery that had taken place in San Francisco two years earlier. Following an extensive manhunt, Franklin had been spotted and arrested in Paso Robles three months ago, and subsequently had been transferred and held in San Francisco to await trial there.

Unaware of his capture and forthcoming trial, everyone in Palm Springs believed that Simon Franklin had killed John. Now everyone would know that was impossible.

Mandy's reaction was milder than I expected. "That means Martha Mae identified the wrong person after John was shot." Strictly speaking, her statement was true, as we both knew.

"As far as anyone else knows, Simon is the only person who had any reason to kill John," I said. "John was mean and spiteful, but that's not much of a motive for murder."

"No motive, no suspects."

"As far as anyone else knows," I said again.

"Yes. We're the only ones who know that John threatened to kill the lot of us."

My train of thought followed an obvious but uncomfortable path. "That means we all have a motive—you, me, Martha Mae and Laura. We are the only logical suspects."

"So it seems." Her voice was calm.

"We need to...to..." I threw out my arms in exasperation. "We need to do something."

She slammed her fist on the table. "And just what do you propose, April? If your supposition is correct, and it probably is, then what do you suggest we do?"

"I don't know." My voice cracked. "I don't know what to do." I curled up into a ball in the overstuffed chair.

Within moments, Mandy was kneeling in front of me, stroking my hair. "I'll tell you this," she said softly. "I swear to you that I didn't kill John. And I know that you didn't do it, either."

"That's enough, then." I took her hands in mine. "When it comes out that Martha Mae could not have seen Simon at the murder scene, people probably will assume that it was simply a case of mistaken identity."

She nodded. "Hopefully, it will end there; one more unsolved murder that will soon be forgotten."


IT DIDN'T END there. Almost everywhere I went, I overheard people discussing the fact that Simon Franklin had been incarcerated at the time John was killed. As far as I could tell, it was generally accepted that Martha Mae had made an honest mistake in her belief that she had seen Simon at the murder scene. The conclusion was inescapable, therefore, that the killer was still at large.

The townspeople began to cast about for suspects. Unaware of John's threat against them, nobody considered the possibility that either Laura or Martha Mae might be the murderer. Nevertheless, they became openly hostile toward both women.

For the first few weeks after John's death, Laura was met with kindness and sympathy everywhere she went. She terminated her employment at the dry goods store. She hired Frank Borner, whose skill as a gunsmith was known and respected, to operate Palm Valley Hardware and Supply. All went well until it became widely known and widely discussed that Laura spent every possible moment with notorious "lady of the evening" Martha Mae Kellogg.

Martha Mae's life was unchanged. As always, most men were drawn to her striking good looks and irresistible charm. Most women avoided her. But for Laura, the new regime was traumatic.

As the wife of a successful business owner, Laura had never given much thought to matters relating to her social status or the respect of her peers. She had never participated or had an interest in gossip and scandals involving others. Now she found herself a social outcast.

People she had known for years turned away to avoid her when she approached them. She imagined the worst—that they knew she and Martha Mae were lovers. Mandy assured her that such a concept was well beyond the grasp of the gossipmongers, and that the most scandalous situation they were capable of concocting was that Laura had fallen under Martha Mae's evil spell and soon would follow her down the road to ruin.

Laura's moods began to shift rapidly from one extreme to another. For the first time in her life, she was deeply in love and sexually fulfilled. But she began to dread leaving her house and encountering the stares and rejection of people she had once counted among her friends. It soon became evident to Martha Mae that they should leave Palm Springs.


MANDY AND I were encountering problems of our own. It began when the social column of the Banning Herald announced the forthcoming arrival of Kenneth and Mabel Kent of Weaver's Flat, Arizona. They planned to spend two months at the home of Mrs. Kent's brother and sister-in-law, Frank and Dora Borner. Mr. Borner, readers were reminded, had recently assumed the position of manager of Palm Valley Hardware and Supply.

Our past seemed to be chasing us and closing in from multiple directions. Perhaps it was coincidence. Or perhaps Palm Springs was too small to live in anonymously. Whatever the reason, we felt uncomfortable. It became evident that it was in our best interest to leave as well.


"WE HAVE TO get out of here." Mandy looked around the kitchen table at each of us. There was no disagreement. "I was such a fool to think we would never be noticed or discovered in a small town."

Martha Mae said, "I suppose Laura and I could go to Tucson. I've kept in touch with Kitty Cole." She looked at Mandy. "As you know, Kitty took Lurline McCann to Tucson from the Yuma Prison. Hank Edwards and the girls still have the house there and—"

"I don't want to do that," Laura said.

Martha Mae smiled. "Truth be told, I don't want to either. In fact, I've been thinking a lot lately about retiring." She touched her cheek. "I'm not getting any younger."

I had often wondered why Martha Mae continued to pursue her profession. Thanks to Jakey and the Lost Dutchman Mine, she and Mandy had more money than they would ever need.

"We could go to a big city," Martha Mae said. "We could all go together...maybe to San Francisco or Los Angeles."

Laura said, "John's brother Albert lives in Los Angeles. I got a condolence letter from him just last week. He says I'm welcome to come and stay with his family on their ranch."

"I'm not well suited for ranch life," Martha Mae said.

Laura laughed. "This isn't a typical ranch. It's thirteen thousand acres."

"Thirteen thousand?" Mandy asked.

"Yes, in cattle and wheat. He has over sixty barns, and he employs hundreds of workers, as you can imagine." She glanced at Martha Mae. "He has a huge ranch house, and he serves meals to seventy workers in one sitting."

Martha Mae's face brightened. "It sounds almost like a little village. I might like it there."

Laura said, "I'll write a letter to Albert." She looked at Mandy, then at me. "If he agrees to it, would you like to accompany us?"

Although I knew the answer, it was difficult to accept. We had lived in Palm Springs for almost three years. We owned a home that was filled with possessions we had acquired during that time. Our situation was far more complicated than it had been when we left Arizona with almost nothing. Still, the conclusion was unavoidable.

"That sounds like a strong possibility," I said. Mandy nodded in agreement.

We spent the next hour working out the contents of the letter Laura would write to her brother-in-law. She would ask that he provide temporary accommodations for three ladies who had given her comfort and support after John's death. Their presence would be helpful until she adjusted to her new surroundings. I didn't expect to stay at Albert Workman's ranch for any length of time. But it would provide us with a safe place in Los Angeles until we made permanent arrangements.

UPON RECEIVING ALBERT'S speedy and enthusiastic reply, we set to work preparing for our move. Thanks to an advertisement in the Banning Herald, we sold our house almost immediately. The purchasers, a family from Chicago, also needed furnishings. For a small additional sum, we agreed to leave them everything except our personal possessions.

We learned that even before our decision to leave the town, Laura had found buyers for both her house and the Palm Valley Hardware and Supply. Shabby treatment and social ostracism had taken their toll. She was happy that her business transactions would be concluded before we moved on.

Our departure was bittersweet. We rode to the train stop in a heavily loaded wagon drawn by two horses and driven by James Collier. Daisy and the mule were tethered to the rear, bearing only the weight of their empty saddles. It seemed a lifetime ago that we had arrived here and walked the six mile road into town while the animals carried everything we owned.

James helped load the animals and luggage. Then it was time for the final goodbye. Although we were relieved to be on our way, we were emotionally shaken. Even James's eyes were moist.

The train pulled away moments after we climbed aboard. I looked back and watched as James turned the wagon and headed slowly back to town. I realized that I would never see any of it again. The Indian children who were so dear to me, our lovely home, the friends we had made...for the rest of my life Palm Springs would be merely a memory.

# Chapter Twelve
## Los Angeles, California, 1891

IT WAS LATE afternoon when the train arrived at our destination, a stop called Chatsworth Park. To our surprise, a wagon was there to meet us. Per Albert Workman's instructions, the driver loaded our luggage and tethered Daisy and the mule to the rear. He told us that the Workman Ranch was nearby.

Soon we were surrounded by wheat fields, and then the ranch house came into view. It was a huge structure, built using adobe and redwood lumber. As we approached, Albert appeared and ran to greet us. Like his deceased brother, he was a big, burly man with a heavy Australian accent. But the resemblance ended there. Albert smiled when he spoke, and his eyes sparkled.

He went directly to Laura and helped her down from the wagon. "I'm so happy you came. There will always be a place at the Workman Ranch for my brother's wife." He looked at each of us and added, "And I'm happy your companions were able to accompany you."

A nagging thought entered my mind: there was a very high probability that his brother's killer was among us. I glanced at Mandy. Although I couldn't be certain of it, her tense expression suggested that she was thinking along the same lines.

Albert instructed the driver to see to the needs of Daisy and the mule. Servants emerged from within the house. They followed behind us, carrying our luggage. Once inside, I was overwhelmed by the scale of the rooms.

From a huge entry with a high ceiling and elaborate ornamentation, a wide staircase led to the guest quarters on the second floor. Albert showed us upstairs. There were several bedrooms furnished with fine European furniture and art. A separate sitting room provided guests with comfortable chairs for reading or relaxing. We were told that wine or tea and biscuits would be brought whenever we wished.

When it became evident that our host had designated four bedrooms for us, Mandy put her hand over her mouth to cover a grin. Of the first four pieces of luggage on the landing, we indicated that each was to be placed in a different room. After Albert left we sorted it all out...the sleeping arrangements, as well as our possessions. Laura and Martha Mae chose a bedroom and indicated to the servants which luggage was to be placed in it. Mandy and I did the same. Hazel, the upstairs maid, observed in undisguised disgust.

"Do you think the maid will cause trouble for us?" I asked Mandy.

She frowned. "I don't know. But for now this is where I live, and I won't hide my life in my own house."

Too excited to relax and refresh ourselves, we went downstairs to explore the remainder of the magnificent house. The dining room for the ranch workers occupied most of the rear portion of the lower floor. Long wooden tables with benches on each side could accommodate several dozen people.

All ranch business was conducted in several rooms near the front of the house that served as offices. Many were nicely furnished with Indian art, massive bookcases, and large desks with ornate wooden chairs. Others were spartan, equipped only with simple writing desks, file cabinets and typewriters. Behind the office area was the Workman family library. I had not seen such an impressive collection of books since leaving the East.

The family dining room was in the center of the house. We had our first meal there the following day. I was unused to such luxury and extravagance. Five courses of California-Spanish cuisine were served on brilliant china and silver. The final course, a local delicacy, was a freshly picked watermelon that had been kept cool in a tank of water until we were ready for it. It was brought to the table, where Albert cracked it open and sliced off a generous chunk for each guest.

After the meal, we retired to our rooms for the customary midday siesta. We had been introduced to the members of Albert's inner circle, and I was curious to learn if Mandy's impressions of them matched my own. Her opinions of some of the guests were, I thought, quite harsh. But as usual, her remarkable insight into human nature would be showcased during the next few months.

The huge bed was soft and comfortable. As we lay on our backs and stared at the ceiling, we grew drowsy. I rolled onto my side and put my arm around Mandy's waist.

"Do you think we'll be all right?" I asked.

Her eyes were closed. "We're safe for now. I'm certain of it."

I stroked her forearm gently. She dozed off.


ALBERT WAS A widower. His wife, a woman called Henrietta Feliz who came from a prominent Los Angeles family, had died in 1889. He had two surviving sons, both of whom had attended Harvard University. Upon graduation, both relocated to New York City, where each had achieved notable success — one as a high ranking executive in the investment banking and brokerage firm of Hornblower & Weeks, the other as a member of the Board of Directors of the New York Stock Exchange. Although Albert was proud of their achievements, he was disheartened by their complete lack of interest in pursuing the family business.

Only after the death of his wife did Albert acknowledge the existence of his illegitimate daughter, Carlotta Tipton, who immediately changed her legal name to Workman. Six months to the day after

Henrietta's funeral, he invited Carlotta, then aged nineteen, to join the daily family meal at the Workman Ranch. She was not well received by the staff. Stigmatized by her peers as a bastard child, her years as an outcast had made her bitter toward everyone around her, and toward Albert in particular.

Carlotta would have been an attractive woman if the hateful, ugly person within had not been reflected in her face. So sure was she of her newly granted status as a Workman family member that she did not attempt to disguise her feelings or her motives. She hated Albert. She coveted the Workman Ranch.

The superintendent of the ranch was an ambitious young man called Robert Clayton. His place at dinner was next to the head of the table, at Albert's right side. To Robert's right sat his wife, Irene. The Claytons had moved to Los Angeles from St. Louis, and I knew of Irene Clayton from the society pages there. She belonged to a prominent German family that had made millions in the beer industry.

Although Irene would inherit the bulk of her estate after the death of her parents, she already controlled a considerable fortune of her own. She was a plain-looking woman. Her nose was a bit too long. Her curly brown hair was a bit unruly. She was very thin, and her dress was a bit too large.

Robert treated his wife with courtesy and respect. But his eyes rarely left Carlotta, who was seated opposite him. I was seated on Carlotta's immediate left, which enabled me to observe their interaction. Irene apparently was oblivious to the situation. Carlotta thoroughly enjoyed Robert's attention. Robert pressed on, unaware that his flirtations were observed by others.

During the first month of our stay, Mandy and I found ways to contribute to the operation of the ranch. Both of us provided much-needed help in typewriting the many letters and invoices that were required in the course of day-to-day business. Mandy tried to help with bookkeeping chores, but her efforts were continually hampered by Albert's head accountant, an unpleasant man named Peter Blaylock.

"Blaylock gets angry whenever anyone goes near the accounting ledgers," she told me. "Albert has no reservations about his integrity, but I suspect that he's hiding something. I don't trust him."

We decided that if Albert was satisfied with the situation, then it was best left alone. Peter Blaylock remained the only person with firsthand knowledge of the financial dealings of the Workman Ranch.

For once, Martha Mae was content to ignore her admirers, including Albert. She and Laura spent happy hours together exploring the ranch and surrounding areas of the rapidly growing San Fernando Valley.


IRENE CLAYTON SOUGHT out my friendship. At first we spoke only of our common experiences in St. Louis. Then one day the neutral subject matter changed. She found me where I spent much of my leisure time — in Albert's magnificent library.

She began with an observation. "You seem quite happy here."

"Oh, I am. I love this area."

"You plan to stay here, then?" she asked.

"Not at the Workman Ranch. But yes, Mandy and I will probably find a place to live here in the San Fernando Valley." I shrugged. "We didn't intend to stay with Albert as long as we have."

"He'll be sorry to see you go. He's well aware of how much you and Mandy contribute to the operation of the ranch." She smiled. "You've made Robert's job easier, as well."

"Robert told you that?"

Her smile disappeared. "No. It's just my observation. Actually...Robert and I don't discuss much of anything."

I was at a loss for a reply, so I said nothing. After a few awkward moments, she continued.

"The fact is, and I've only recently admitted it to myself, I married Robert only so that I could escape from my dictatorial family." Her eyes grew moist. "I was never actually in love with him, nor was he with me."

"It must be difficult for you." It was all I could think of to say in light of her dreadfully sad revelation.

"It's unbearable, actually. I no longer trust Robert. Even before our first wedding anniversary, I reached the inescapable conclusion that he had wed me not for love, but only for money."

I was shaken. "Irene, I don't know what—"

"Our finances became a ridiculous, tangled mess. My attorney in St. Louis helped me file divorce papers just before we left. Then Robert pressured me to come to California." She shook her head. "He made veiled threats about forcing me back into my parents' custody if I went through with the divorce. At this point, I'm not even certain that we're still married."

"Does it really matter?" I didn't mean to sound disapproving, but apparently I did.

She leaned toward me. "I don't know, and I don't care. I'm relegated to a life of unhappiness no matter what I do. If I stay here, I'll live out my life with a man I've grown to hate. If I return to St. Louis, I'll never escape the stigma of divorce, nor the iron-fisted control of my family."

Again, I was at a loss for a response. "I see," was all I could muster.

She slumped back against her chair. "Besides, Robert and Carlotta are having an affair."

I strongly suspected that she was correct. "Do you have proof?"

"Proof?" She laughed bitterly. "They don't even have the decency to hide their feelings. Surely you've seen their little...display...countless times."

"What do you intend to do?" I asked.

"I don't know."

WHEN I TOLD Mandy about my conversation with Irene, she raised her eyebrows and looked at the ceiling. "'Oh, what a tangled web we weave, when first we practice to deceive.'" Then she winked at me and said, "Sir Walter Scott. Quite perceptive of him, don't you think?"

Even after all the time we had known each other, the extent of Mandy's classical education and analytical abilities sometimes surprised me. But in this case, I wondered if she was off the mark.

"I'm not certain this particular web is so tangled," I said. "As Irene pointed out, we've all observed the flirtations between her husband and Carlotta Workman."

She nodded. "That's exactly my point. Robert and Carlotta are showing all of us what they want us to see. There's something complex going on under the surface, a web of deceit that we're not supposed to know about. I can't quite work it out. Perhaps Martha Mae can shed some light on the matter."

ON THE FOLLOWING Saturday, we joined Laura and Martha Mae for a picnic. From Albert's well-stocked kitchen, they had selected a delicious assortment of bread, cheese, fresh fruit and wine. We put the food and two blankets into baskets, which we carried to a large tree about a half mile south of the main house.

We spread out the blankets under the tree. Laura told us that the tree, called eucalyptus, was not a native of California. In fact, it was Albert who had imported the seeds from Australia several years earlier, and he was solely responsible for the plethora of eucalyptus trees in the area.

As we began to unpack the picnic baskets, Mandy looked at Martha Mae and asked, "What do you think Robert Clayton and Carlotta Workman are plotting?"

I was surprised that she asked the question. Although I had not been able to put the situation out of my mind, I had no intention of bringing it up at the picnic.

Martha Mae smiled. "I've given that matter considerable thought. The problem seems to revolve around Robert. He's not an honorable man."

"I agree," Laura said. "His blatant flirtations with Carlotta are absolutely —"

"No, I don't mean that." Martha Mae waved her hand dismissively. "I'm referring to the deception he's perpetrating on Carlotta. She thinks he loves her, and he doesn't."

"Irene would disagree vehemently with that observation," I said.

Martha Mae picked out an orange from one of our baskets and

studied it. "Irene believes that Robert ignores her because he's interested in Carlotta romantically." She fell silent and appeared to concentrate on peeling the orange.

"And?" I asked impatiently.

"And Robert ignores Irene because he has no interest in her. She's correct about that. However, he doesn't care much for Carlotta, either. His interest is in Carlotta's money."

"That makes no sense," Mandy said. "Irene is the one with all the money. She's an heiress. Carlotta has almost nothing, and she'll have no appreciable wealth of her own until Albert dies and...oh."

"Do you think Albert is in danger?" Laura asked.

"Not at the moment, if Robert has any say in the matter," Martha Mae said.

Mandy was irritated. "You're going in circles. You're speaking nonsense."

Martha Mae threw back her head and laughed heartily. "Oh, Mandy, for such an intelligent woman you understand so little about the mental gymnastics of the male of our species." She paused, then added, "In my business, that knowledge is essential."

"Please dispense your great wisdom," Mandy said sarcastically.

"In a nutshell, Robert intends to commandeer Irene's fortune. Then he intends to marry Carlotta, who will eventually be quite wealthy, and in all likelihood will control the Workman Ranch."

"Commandeer?" Mandy asked. "Do you believe that Irene's life is in danger?"

"His scheme won't work," I said. "Irene told me she's already filed for divorce. Her intention is to give Robert absolutely nothing."

Martha Mae frowned. "I hope the divorce is finalized while she's still alive."

I had never known Martha Mae to be wrong in matters concerning human nature. Once again, her theory seemed to make sense. The facts had been in front of me for weeks, and I hadn't connected them properly.

Like Mandy and Laura, I found the situation profoundly disturbing. We finished the picnic in somber silence and walked back to the main house.

# Chapter Thirteen

MINDFUL OF MARTHA Mae's insight into the situation, I viewed Robert's behavior at our daily dinner in a new light. Nuances that had escaped my notice earlier became obvious to me. However, both Irene and Carlotta appeared to believe the façade that Robert presented. The routine changed one day when Albert announced that Robert would be leaving shortly for a one-week business trip in San Francisco.

Wheat output on the ranch had increased markedly due to improved irrigation and the cultivation of several hundred additional acres. Fortunately, demand had also increased, particularly in the northern part of the state. Albert sought to establish a contract with the Sperry Flour Company, a large successful mill in San Francisco. He delegated the task of negotiating the contract to Robert.

On the following Monday, a wagon driven by one of the ranch hands delivered Robert to the Chatsworth Park stop, where he boarded the northbound train. Because of this, I looked forward to a week of more enjoyable dinners. But it was not to be.

At the first dinner without Robert, the animosity between Irene and Carlotta was on display for all to see. Although neither woman had acknowledged the other while Robert was present, they glared viciously at one another in his absence.

Albert grew uncomfortable and asked to speak to Carlotta in private. They stepped out of the room for a few moments. When they returned, Carlotta's face was flushed with anger. She avoided looking at Irene, and focused instead on the dinner table. When Albert smiled at Irene and nodded, she did the same.

On the second day of Robert's absence, dinner proceeded smoothly. As usual, we chatted about world news that had been reported in the Los Angeles Times, as well as local activities and events. Both Irene and Carlotta were totally silent throughout the meal, which was typical.


THE NEXT DAY Irene was absent from the dinner table. Albert summoned the ranch foreman, a man called Eduardo Gomez, and dispatched him to the Clayton bungalow to try to locate Irene. We turned our attention to the meal and the usual banter after Eduardo left. About twenty minutes later he returned, ashen-faced.

"Did you locate Mrs. Clayton?" Albert asked.

Eduardo's voice trembled. "I found her at her home. She is dead. Someone killed her with a knife."

The room fell silent. Albert's face was grim. He stood and instructed the headwaiter to clear the table, then nodded toward us and left without a word. Albert's two assistants and Carlotta followed. The servants removed the remainder of the meal and disappeared, leaving only the four of us: Martha Mae, Laura, Mandy and me.

"This is terribly disconcerting," Laura said. "I almost feel responsible, since we were talking only a few days ago about whether Irene's life was in danger. And now...poor, sweet Irene."

I, too, found the matter most distressing. Irene and I had begun to form a friendship of the type I imagined two sisters might share.

Mandy said, "The Claytons' bungalow is less than a hundred yards from here. I wonder if anyone heard any suspicious noises coming from that direction today."

I said, "Perhaps she inadvertently interrupted a burglar. The Claytons have a great deal of valuable jewelry and silver. And it's no secret around the ranch that Robert is out of town."

"Perhaps." Mandy knitted her eyebrows. "But everyone connected with the ranch knows that Irene always comes to the main house for midday dinner. A burglar would probably have waited until she left the bungalow."

"If she interrupted a burglary in progress, the house will be at least partly disheveled," Martha Mae said. She paused a moment then added, "unless it was a deliberate murder that was set up to look like merely a burglary."

Laura stood and said, "I think we should go over to the Claytons' bungalow."

"I don't believe Albert would want us there at the moment, sweetheart," Martha Mae said.

Laura smiled. "Leave Albert to me. Let's go."


ALBERT STOOD WITH his back to us, whispering to the sheriff, in the parlor of the Claytons' bungalow. On the couch a few feet away was Irene's body, apparently untouched since Eduardo had discovered it.

It appeared that nothing in the room had been disturbed. Laura slipped out quietly and returned moments later. When she shook her head slightly, I understood that the rest of the residence was in order. It was a straightforward case of murder.

None of us had uttered a word since we had entered, so Albert was surprised when he turned and saw us. "You ladies should not be here," he said. His tone was soft and gentle, but it was clear that remaining was not an option.

We walked back to the main house and found it empty as expected, since the servants had returned to their quarters for the midday siesta. Confident that our conversation would not be overheard, we assembled in the library.

"This whole thing makes no sense at all," Laura said.

Mandy shook her head. "Someone had a motive. *Cui bono?*"

"What did you say?" I asked.

"*Cui bono*? Who benefits? Who gains from Irene's death?"

I thought for a moment. "Nobody...unless..."

Martha Mae anticipated where my thoughts were headed. "You've already told us the answer, April," she said impatiently. "Robert will inherit her fortune, unless her divorce from him is already final."

Mandy said, "Wait a moment. Let's unravel the facts." She looked at me. "Tell us once again what you know about this divorce."

"Irene told me that she saw an attorney before they left St. Louis. She said she asked him to file for her divorce from Robert and she signed all the necessary papers. She also had him draw up a revised will."

"Did she tell you the name of the attorney?"

"No."

Mandy frowned. "This is tricky. If that revised will is found, I have a feeling it will cost Robert a bundle. And if, as I suspect, their divorce was granted before Irene's death, it will also cost him whatever the State of California would have considered their community property."

"It certainly appears that Robert is the prime suspect...in fact, the only suspect," Laura said.

Martha Mae said, "Yes, and he's also the one person who has an ironclad alibi. Don't forget, he's in San Francisco."

"Supposedly," Laura said.

Martha Mae raised her eyebrows. "It's possible that he got off the northbound train at the first stop and returned here a few hours later."

Mandy said, "We can verify his presence in San Francisco by telegraph. I'll go into town and send a wire."

"My dear Robert," said Martha Mae with a mischievous grin, "Your wife has been murdered. Did you kill her, or are you actually there in San Francisco?"

Mandy rolled her eyes. "Your sense of humor is perverse."

"Nonsense. It's these man-woman people who are perverse, not my sense of humor. Trust me."

"Since it's your business to know such things, naturally I trust you," Mandy said playfully. Then she turned to me. "Can you find out where Robert planned to stay in San Francisco?"

I nodded. I knew exactly where to look.

GILES WIMBERLY HANDLED all ranch transactions related to monetary expenditures. His job involved a great deal of typewriting and filing, so in my capacity as a volunteer clerical helper, it was not at all unusual for me to be in his office and handling his files. Nevertheless, I worked as quickly as I could, so that I would not be present when Giles returned from the midday siesta.

I delivered the information to Mandy. A reservation had been made for Robert for six days at the Palace, a magnificent new hotel with over seven hundred luxury rooms.

Mandy headed for the stable immediately. She would ride Daisy into the village center, send her wire, and hope for a quick reply. Although the old horse had worked only rarely in the last few years, she still enjoyed it. Mandy watched her carefully. When the day came that carrying her mistress was more a burden than a pleasure, Daisy would retire permanently to a life of leisure.

Horse and rider returned before dark. The response had been received less than two hours after the inquiry was sent. A man giving the name of Robert Clayton had checked into San Francisco's Palace Hotel three days earlier. He had not checked out.

"Then Robert could not have killed Irene," I said.

Mandy shrugged. "It's unlikely that anyone went to San Francisco in Robert's place. We'll learn more when he returns with the wheat contracts he's negotiated. Those papers will bear his signature and a date."

It would be a simple matter for me to find a document with Robert's signature on file in the office. I didn't expect to find an inconsistency with the signature on the new contracts he was to deliver at the end of the week, but I knew it was a possibility.


UNDER ALBERT'S PERSONAL supervision, Irene's remains were taken by wagon to a mortuary in Los Angeles. The sheriff locked the bungalow and posted a notice on the door that entry was prohibited. No other action would occur until Albert met Robert's train at the Chatsworth Park stop when he returned.

For the rest of the week, the midday dinners were strained. Irene's empty chair was a painful reminder of our loss. Even worse was Carlotta's attitude. For the first time since I had met her, she smiled contentedly throughout each meal. On several occasions, I noticed her smile widen a bit when she glanced at Irene's chair. Carlotta's deplorable behavior angered me. It was obvious that she intended to reap great rewards for herself and Robert as a result of Irene's death. I resolved to do everything in my power to prevent it.

After Robert returned with the wheat contracts, I verified his signature. My small glimmer of hope vanished. He had in fact been in San Francisco on the day his wife died.


RONALD GRESHAM WAS not my favorite cousin, by far. As children, our animosity toward one another was blatant. As adults, we barely managed to treat each other with civility. When I left St. Louis, I had no intention of having contact with Ronald for the remainder of my life. However, he had become a prominent attorney and it was likely that he could find the information I sought.

I took a deep breath and began to write a letter to him. I opened, of course, with the usual salutations and comments regarding family matters. Then I explained my unusual request. I was involved in a very delicate matter related to a dear friend from St. Louis who had recently died. Unfortunately, I had neglected to ask her for the name of her attorney. Could Ronald make discrete inquiries and procure that information for me? If so, I would be most grateful. Although it was admittedly somewhat hypocritical, I signed the letter, "Your loving cousin, April."

My letter to Ronald went out with the morning post. Considering our stormy past relationship, I didn't have much hope that my cousin would try to find the answer to my question, or even that he would give me the courtesy of a reply. I was shocked when his response arrived a month later.

Ronald had known the answer before he received my letter. Irene's attorney was one of the senior partners in his own firm—a man called Ernest Jarvis. The Law Offices of Colby, Saxton and Jarvis had handled all legal matters for Irene's family for over twenty years. Mr. Jarvis himself had received an inquiry regarding Irene from an attorney in California whom Irene had retained. The man's name was Arthur Vonzell, and his office was located in Los Angeles on South Broadway between Second and Third Streets.

In the five weeks since Irene died, Robert had neglected many of his duties and spent long hours tracking down various parts of her fortune. Although two local attorneys were involved due to the size and complexity of the estate, the possibility of a divorce or a revised will had never been considered.

I showed my cousin's letter to Mandy. Her strong opinion was that we should visit Mr. Vonzell at the earliest possible moment. We left for his office the next morning at first light.


ARTHUR VONZELL WAS a small, thin man in his late thirties with sparse blond hair. He wore round wire-rimmed spectacles and a bow tie. After our introductions, he offered us two guest chairs and took his own seat, a leather upholstered executive chair on the opposite side of his large mahogany desk.

"How might I be of assistance to you ladies?" he asked.

I drew Ronald's letter from my handbag. "My cousin is an attorney with Colby, Saxton and Jarvis in St. Louis," I said. "Mr. Ernest Jarvis has indicated that he sent you material regarding Mrs. Irene Clayton, and that you may have developed additional material for her."

He nodded. "Yes, I've done some work for Mrs. Clayton."

His tone indicated that he was reluctant to provide details. I couldn't blame him. I was, after all, a complete stranger to him. I wasn't certain how to proceed. Fortunately, Mandy intervened.

"I believe you drafted Mrs. Clayton's Last Will and Testament," she said. "Can you tell us if it was recorded, and do you happen to have a copy on hand?"

I surmised her strategy. We had no idea whether the will existed, but by presuming knowledge of it we might eliminate Mr. Vonzell's reservations about discussing the matter. Her ploy was successful. His face relaxed.

"It isn't a common practice, but Mrs. Clayton's will was recorded about three months ago, along with..." He stopped abruptly.

"Yes? Along with what?" Mandy asked.

His mantle of reluctance returned. "I'm afraid I'm not at liberty to discuss—"

"Her divorce?" I interjected.

I was guessing that he would be willing to discuss any aspect of Irene's personal business, provided that we were already aware of it. It appeared that my guess was correct. His face relaxed again.

"Yes. Mrs. Clayton's divorce was finalized in St. Louis after the Claytons left for California. She engaged me to obtain a copy of the divorce decree and record it for her in Los Angeles...just to be on the safe side."

Mandy said, "Mr. Vonzell, let me make sure that I understand this. Irene Clayton's final divorce decree and her most recent Last Will and Testament have both been recorded in Los Angeles County. Is that correct?"

"Yes."

"Can you give us a letter to that effect?"

He hesitated. "You see, there is considerable expense associated with drafting a letter and—"

"Let me ask a different question," Mandy said with a smile. "Might I retain you to draft a letter to that effect?"

"Certainly."

We watched as he scribbled out the information. He read the draft, made two changes, and nodded in satisfaction. He stepped through a door in the back of the room and returned moments later, telling us that his secretary would prepare the letter promptly.

Within a half hour, a small, thin middle-aged woman with sparse white hair and round wire-rimmed spectacles emerged. She smiled at us briefly and placed two copies of Mr. Vonzell's letter, typewritten under his letterhead, on his desk.

After Mandy paid his fee, Mr. Vonzell signed one of the copies, placed it in an envelope, and slid it across the desk toward us. I placed it in my handbag.

Minutes later, we were on our way back to the Workman Ranch. I was uncertain as to how we should proceed.

As if she had read my mind, Mandy said, "I think it's time for us to speak with Albert."

# Chapter Fourteen

LAURA WAS WAITING for us. The moment we came through the front door, she motioned for us to follow her to the library. There we found Martha Mae seated in a huge Queen Anne chair, leafing through an illustrated volume of great European paintings. She closed the book abruptly when we entered.

Mandy said, "We were more successful than I dared hope, in terms of finding useful information." She sat in the chair opposite Martha Mae and stretched out her legs. "Now the question is, how best to use it."

"What did you learn?" Martha Mae asked.

"Irene was divorced from Robert, and she made a new will shortly before she died," Mandy said.

"We obtained a letter from her attorney in Los Angeles verifying that the relevant documents have been recorded," I added.

Martha Mae whistled. "The future doesn't look bright for Robert. Carlotta won't be happy, either."

Laura said, "The way Carlotta constantly gushes over Robert is truly disgusting. It's difficult for me to eat dinner at the same table."

"At least he has the decency to pretend that he doesn't notice," I said. "Perhaps he has just a tiny bit of respect for Irene's memory."

"Perhaps he simply doesn't care for Carlotta as much as she believes," Martha Mae said with a laugh.

Mandy said, "Regardless of his feelings about Carlotta, he's been working diligently to confiscate Irene's fortune for himself. We must act quickly if we hope to stop him."

I nodded. "We need to tell Albert what we've learned. We need his help."

There was no disagreement. Laura left the library to search for her brother-in-law. They returned twenty minutes later. Although he was a kind and patient man, the expression on Albert's face indicated that he was not pleased to have his afternoon's work interrupted.

"We want to call your attention to a serious problem," Mandy told him. "It involves Robert Clayton."

Albert remained composed for the most part, but a slight twitch at his right cheek betrayed his aggravation. "If the problem involves Robert, then you should speak directly to Robert."

"I want you to read this," I said. I handed him the letter that Arthur Vonzell had written.

I watched his face as he read. When he finished, he pursed his lips and read it again. His gaze rose to the ceiling, and I saw his anger.

"I believed that Robert was an honorable man. I see now that I misjudged him."

I said, "The immediate concern is the disposition of Irene's estate. Robert has made considerable progress in procuring — "

"No, April, the immediate concern is how to remove Robert without harming the ranch." Albert's eyes blazed. "He has considerable knowledge of this operation, which he could use to our detriment. I must be sure to eliminate his ability to hurt us before I act further."

"That won't be a simple matter," I said. "Judging from the paperwork I've seen in the office, at least half of the business transactions for the ranch involve Robert in one way or another."

He nodded. "I must also think of my daughter. Carlotta is quite fond of Robert, as you must know. If she were to become romantically involved with him it would be...unfortunate."

Martha Mae, seated only a few feet from Albert, reached over and covered his hand with her own. Although it was obvious to me that she was about to speak of Carlotta, I had no idea what she would say. I held my breath.

"I don't want to cause you pain," she said softly. "But the fact is that Carlotta and Robert have been engaged in a physical relationship since the day after Irene's funeral."

He jerked back. "That can't be! How can you say such a thing?"

"I've seen the evidence myself. As you know, my bedroom overlooks the path between this house and Robert's bungalow." She looked earnestly into his eyes and continued. "I'm a light sleeper. In my business...that is, I used to be engaged in an occupation that required me to be alert for long hours at a stretch. I developed a habit of coming fully awake at the slightest sound."

"And you've seen something?" he asked weakly.

She nodded. "I've seen it from my window many times. I won't try to trivialize it. Carlotta leaves this house every night around midnight. Just before first light, she returns."

He buried his head in his hands. "Carlotta. Oh, Carlotta." After a few moments, he composed himself and looked up at Martha Mae. "Are you certain it's Carlotta?"

"I'm certain. You can verify it for yourself. Simply secrete yourself beneath my bedroom window at the times I've given you. You'll see."

He took a deep breath. "Yes. I want to see it for myself. Once I verify it..." he voice broke and he stopped speaking.

Laura got up from her chair and knelt before him. "You're not to blame for this. There's nothing you could have done to prevent it."

He put his hand on her shoulder. "She's brought shame to herself. Don't you see it, Laura? You're a member of this family. She's brought shame to our family, as well."

He stood and left the library without another word.

After he was out of earshot, Mandy looked at Martha Mae and asked, "Why did you keep this to yourself?"

Her tone was unexpectedly agitated. "Because I'm just a bit

sensitive about discussions and moral judgments of other people's personal lives. I've been on the receiving end of that sort of thing hundreds of times. Most of the time, it serves no valid purpose." She softened. "This particular case appears to be different."

I fully understood Martha Mae's resentment of the countless people who had passed judgment on her. But Albert's indignation was not as clear to me. His own behavior outside of his marriage had resulted in Carlotta's birth, and yet he felt intense anger and shame when his daughter engaged in the same indiscretion. I wondered if perhaps one day there would be a single standard for evaluating the conduct of women as opposed to men.

ALBERT PROCEEDED QUICKLY and methodically. Martha Mae reported that she saw him station himself beneath her bedroom window that night. When Carlotta slipped out of the house at midnight, he followed her.

Two days later, three men arrived at the ranch. One of them was familiar to me. He was Deputy Sheriff Carl Jacobsen, who had completed the initial investigation and report of Irene's murder.

Albert introduced the other two men to the staff and explained the reason for their presence. He had employed a private security firm called Pinkerton, and the men were employees of that firm. The first man's assignment was to ensure that Robert Clayton did not gain access to any of the ranch offices. The second man's assignment was to accompany Robert at all times until he removed his personal belongings from his bungalow and vacated the Workman Ranch. He would not be permitted to take anything that might have been owned jointly with his wife. All furnishings, dry goods, dishes, silver and jewelry were to remain in the bungalow until the contents of Irene's newly discovered will were revealed.

Robert's attorney was a man called Francis Kemper, whose office was located in the community of San Fernando, only eleven miles northeast of the ranch. Having been summoned by Albert, Mr. Kemper arrived less than an hour after Sheriff Jacobsen and the private security guards.

I was working nearby at filing invoices when I saw Albert escort Mr. Kemper into his office. To my surprise, he called for Laura to join them. Knowing Albert, I doubted that he thought he needed a witness for the meeting. It was more likely that he felt the need for a sympathetic female family member to assist him in dealing with the more delicate aspects of the situation, specifically, the unfortunate connection between Robert and Carlotta.

Their meeting lasted for only thirty minutes. Mr. Kemper emerged stone-faced. Laura glanced at me, and I could tell in an instant that she was pleased. Albert's face was that of a man on an extremely unpleasant mission.

I DIDN'T HAVE an opportunity to speak with Laura privately before we gathered for dinner. It was a grim affair. Robert's chair, like Irene's, was now empty. I wasn't certain how much Carlotta knew about the events of the last few hours, until she looked at her father. Her hateful glare revealed that she was aware of everything.

"He didn't do anything wrong, Papa."

Albert's eyes met hers. "He lied. He cheated. He tried to steal property that wasn't rightfully his."

"You have no proof," she spat.

"I assure you, I have proof that he did all of those things." He took a deep breath. "I also know that you and Robert have been sharing a bed."

Her face paled. "That isn't true!"

"Don't lie to me." He sounded more hurt than angry. "When I learned of your nightly routine, I couldn't believe it. But recently, I saw it for myself. I followed you to Robert's bungalow. I saw him open the door and...greet you."

"My nightly routine?" Although she was addressing her father, she focused on Mandy. "How could you have learned of my nightly routine?"

I wasn't certain why she thought Mandy had been the one to reveal her affair. If Mandy was surprised, she kept it hidden well. She simply stared back.

Carlotta stood, clutching her napkin tightly, and returned her glare to Albert. "I don't care what you know. You can't keep us apart."

For the first time, there was anger in his voice. "Don't be too certain of that."

"Are you threatening me, Papa?"

He shook his head. "No. But I will tell you that were it not for your future inheritance, Robert would have no interest in you."

She flung her napkin at him. "Damn you, old man!" She scanned the table and screamed, "Damn you all!" She stormed out.

I glanced at Albert. I had never seen him so miserable. His hands trembled, and his eyes were moist. We finished dinner in complete and extremely uncomfortable silence.

Rather than go upstairs to our bedroom as was customary for midday siesta, I drifted aimlessly through the huge house, finally settling in the library. I sat motionless for several minutes in an unsuccessful effort to absorb and understand the disturbing circumstances that surrounded me. I was barely aware of it when Mandy joined me, followed shortly thereafter by Laura and Martha Mae. Apparently I was not alone in my aversion to the thought of a siesta in the midst of chaos.

"What in the world is going to happen?" I asked nobody in particular.

Laura said, "Albert has done everything necessary to protect the ranch. And after his meeting with Francis Kemper this morning, I'm certain that Mr. Kemper will no longer provide Robert with legal assistance in raiding Irene's estate."

"Would Albert actually revoke Carlotta's inheritance, as he inferred?" I asked.

She shook her head. "No, never. But he'll do whatever he can to keep her away from Robert."

Martha Mae said, "That's an interesting thought. If it were to become common knowledge that Albert had decided not to bequeath any of his property to Carlotta, it would be only a matter of time before Robert learned about it."

Mandy grinned at her. "And how do you suppose that might come to pass?"

"I have no idea." Martha Mae leaned back and put her hand on her chest. "I was merely making an observation."

I had known both Mandy and Martha Mae long enough to have learned the peculiar way they communicated with one another. I realized that they had agreed on a plan. Martha Mae would take care of spreading the rumor that Carlotta would inherit none of Albert's estate. Mandy would provide her with any needed assistance.

FOR THE NEXT two days, Carlotta was silent during dinner. She appeared serene. Although Robert was not permitted access to Carlotta or the ranch, he was seen frequently nearby. Apparently she was confident that he would summon her in the near future.

On the third day, her mood was altered radically. She refused to look at any of us, but I could see her bloodshot eyes and puffy face. She picked listlessly at her meal.

I looked at Martha Mae. She smiled innocently — so innocently, in fact, that I knew she had completed her mission to spread the rumor that Carlotta had been disinherited.

Mandy said, "I heard that Robert Clayton left the area yesterday. He's going to Mexico."

Albert nodded. "Yes, I heard the same."

"Papa, is it true that you've disinherited me?" Carlotta asked.

"You are my daughter."

Although his response did not actually answer her question, Carlotta let it pass. Once he believed that Carlotta was not a source of wealth, I guessed that Robert had chosen Mexico as his destination in order to escape any legal problems connected with Irene. And despite Albert's ambivalence, I knew that Carlotta's financial future was secure. What I did not know, and what I intended to find out, was who killed Irene.

# Chapter Fifteen

ROBERT'S EXPULSION FROM the ranch gave me an inexplicable sense of relief. For the next several days, I enjoyed an almost euphoric feeling of well-being. I had once read of such a phenomenon. According to a prominent psychologist, people often require a temporary respite from a trauma of the magnitude of Irene's murder. Although I would not have thought it possible, even our lovemaking was more exciting and fulfilling, much to Mandy's delight.

Carlotta was seen only at dinner. She ate very little and always left the table before the last course was served. Nobody took particular notice on the day she did not appear at all.

The next morning, a housekeeper reported that Carlotta's bed had not been occupied overnight. Albert ordered a thorough search of the ranch. All of her clothing was accounted for. Her horse was in the stable. But Carlotta was gone. When we assembled in the dining room at noon, we found Albert in a state of despair.

He clasped his hands together tightly. "I didn't realize she was so upset that she would run away. I should have paid closer attention."

"You couldn't have anticipated it," Laura said. "Young women in Carlotta's situation rarely react as she did."

Martha Mae said, "That's true. Her reaction is...unusual." Her glance at Mandy indicated that she had more to say about the matter later, when they could speak privately.

We ate in awkward silence. At the end of the meal, we took Martha Mae's cue and followed her to the library. I closed the door behind me.

"Do you think she's pregnant?" Mandy asked without preamble.

Martha Mae said, "If she is, I don't believe she's aware of the fact. In my experience, an unmarried pregnant woman waits until she can't hide it before taking action of any kind."

"Then why would she run away?" I asked.

"To be with Robert."

"In Mexico? How could she hope to travel so far alone, and then to locate Robert?"

She smiled. "That does seem unrealistic, doesn't it? I think we need to examine the idea that Robert did in fact go to Mexico."

It became apparent this so-called "fact" was actually rumor and hearsay. One of the ranch hands was told by a stranger who claimed to be a railroad employee that Robert had gone to Mexico. The news had spread from there. Martha Mae was not surprised.

"Do you think he's here, waiting for Carlotta?" I asked.

She raised her eyebrows. "I'm not sure. But I believe we'll hear something soon."

As usual, Martha Mae was correct.


THE NEXT MORNING, an old Indian woman appeared at the ranch house. She had been paid handsomely to deliver a note to Albert, and she had walked several miles to complete her mission. She insisted on putting the note directly into Albert's hands.

As Laura and I descended the stairs, we saw Albert escorting the woman to the kitchen. We followed. The woman was frightened, and terribly thirsty. She gulped down three glasses of water before she collapsed into a wooden chair and focused on her surroundings.

Albert motioned for the woman to remain seated and handed the note to Laura. I read along with her. It was a thinly veiled attempt at a ransom note.

> Papa, I will be released if you leave two-hundred pounds of gold coins inside the big cave at the south end of Stoney Point at sunset tomorrow. You know the place. Please do not try to interfere with the men who are holding me, as they are exceedingly dangerous. Your loving daughter, Carlotta

The huge rock outcropping called Stoney Point, about six miles north of the ranch, was well known throughout the area. It had been home to the Tongva Indians for centuries. In the current era, it had been used as a hideout for the famous "Robin Hood" outlaw Tiburcio Vasquez in the 1870s.

I slipped out of the kitchen to look for Mandy. I found her in one of the front offices and told her about the note.

She shook her head. "That poor, foolish woman."

"Do you suppose they actually believe that they can trick Albert out of all that gold and live a life of leisure in Mexico?" I asked.

As we walked to the kitchen, Mandy said, "I suspect that's what Carlotta believes. But if Robert were ever to get his hands on a fortune such as that, he would leave her without a second thought."

"You and Albert are in complete agreement," I said. "Still, he wants his daughter back. He believes that Robert will abandon her if he gets the gold that's been demanded."

Mandy nodded. "It might be risky. Robert could keep her with him until he knew for certain that he was safely away from here. Then he might abandon her in the desert, or even kill her."

"Albert is aware of that possibility. He's already sent for Carl Jacobsen. He wants the sheriff's help."

We entered the kitchen as the old Indian woman was about to leave. Albert gave her a handsome reward and ensured that she would be given a ride home on a wagon. He whispered briefly to Mandy as we moved to the dining room for the midday meal. She nodded. I surmised that she was to be included in the plan to rescue Carlotta.

After dinner, I followed Albert and Mandy to the library. He was inclined to exclude me from their meeting, but Mandy insisted that I should stay. We were joined a few minutes later by Sheriff Jacobsen.

Albert summarized the situation. For those familiar with Stoney Point, there was no question as to the location of the huge cave Carlotta had specified in her note.

"Sheriff, have you ever heard the tale about another entrance to that cave?" Albert asked.

He nodded. "It's more than a tale. We located it quite by accident several years ago, before the railroad came in. We were tracking down three men who had held up the stagecoach that used to go past there. We came upon them just as they were emerging from a small opening on the other side of the rocks. We crawled in and found a shaft that led to the big cave."

"Could Robert Clayton possibly know about that entrance?" Mandy asked.

"Based on the demand in the note, my guess is that he does," Jacobsen said. "Once Albert leaves the gold inside the main entrance, Robert and Carlotta probably plan to haul it through the shaft and out the other side, where they won't be seen."

Mandy said, "We can assume that Robert will work with Carlotta until he has no further use for her. That means one of them will watch Albert's approach to the cave, and the other will be inside to ensure that the gold delivery meets their demand."

"My guess is that Carlotta will be inside the cave," Albert said.

Jacobsen said, "Yes, I believe Robert plans to hide nearby and watch as the gold is delivered. He'll want to know if Albert has brought other men along, and if so, how many. Then he intends to slip around to the back side of the rocks and move his booty out from there."

Mandy said, "Sheriff, I believe that if Albert and I take the gold to the cave on a wagon, Robert won't be alarmed. The presence of a woman shouldn't bother him. Once Carlotta sees the gold coins, she'll undoubtedly send a signal from the cave entrance that the treasure is in her possession."

He nodded. "I can post some of my men at the back side. We can apprehend him when he comes around."

Albert said, "I don't like this plan. It puts my daughter in too much danger."

I could not hold my tongue. "You know that the greatest danger Carlotta faces comes from Robert. The entire purpose of the plan is to separate her from him."

I realized that I sounded angry. In reality, I was frightened, not only for Mandy, but for all of them. I had gradually come to understand that Robert Clayton was a vicious man who cared nothing for anyone except himself. Now he was a desperate man as well. I feared that he would stop at nothing.

After my outburst, the tone of their discussion changed. They focused on specific details. Sheriff Jacobsen was to post three of his men out of sight behind the cave near the hidden entrance. Mandy's pistol would be wrapped in a blanket, hidden underneath her feet on the floor of the wagon. Albert would be unarmed. Jacobsen himself would follow on horseback about a mile behind the wagon. Upon a signal from Mandy of two gunshots, he would ride in quickly to help.

They were ready. Now all there was to do was wait until sunset of the following day.

THE SHERIFF AND his deputies arrived at the ranch late in the afternoon. A wagon and two-horse team had been readied for the trip. A wooden ammunition box behind the driver's seat held ten canvas bags of gold coins, each weighing twenty pounds. Although not a considerable fortune by most standards, it was probably all a single thief could carry if he hoped to escape on horseback.

I watched with trepidation as they left. Albert and Mandy led the way in the wagon, followed by the four lawmen on their horses. When they were out of sight, I wandered through the garden. Then I began to walk the perimeter of the house, moving slowly and staring at the ground. On my third cycle, Martha Mae came outside and asked me if something was wrong.

We sat in a big swing on the verandah and rocked gently. As I began to talk to her, I realized that my concerns extended far beyond the current crisis with Carlotta.

"What's going to happen to us?" I asked. "We don't belong here. Even Laura doesn't belong here...not really."

She gazed at the nearby wheat fields. "I've also been thinking along those lines. Albert would be perfectly happy to have all of us stay, especially you and Mandy, since you do so much of the office work. But...."

"It doesn't feel right," I said. "I don't want to spend the rest of my days living in someone else's house. I want a home with Mandy, like we had in Palm Springs."

She nodded. "I understand. I suppose that since money isn't a problem for Mandy or me, it's merely a matter of determining what we want to do with our lives."

"For me, I believe it would be teaching children," I said. "I think often of Palm Springs and the Indian children in my little class. I so enjoyed them."

Martha Mae said, "The only school I'm aware of in this area is located at Lopez Station. They might have a need for someone with your skills."

I knew of the place. It was an old stagecoach stop that housed the area's first post office, as well as the first English-speaking school. It was located about ten miles east of the ranch.

"I need to discuss this with Mandy," I said. "I want to settle down someplace permanently. But I'm not certain as to where we should go. It's difficult."

Martha Mae rested her hand on her chin, apparently deep in thought. "I recently read about something that may interest you. A railroad station is planned at the Chatsworth Park train stop. They envision it as a significant station, including a diner, telegraph office, and even a hotel adjacent to it."

The Los Angeles Times had printed a small article about the plan. The Southern Pacific Railroad had enjoyed ever increasing passenger traffic on the line between Los Angeles and San Francisco. Chatsworth Park, a natural stopping point along the way, had even begun to attract permanent settlers. I could easily imagine that one day soon a small village might spring up in the area.

Having grown up in St. Louis, I knew that city life no longer suited me. But life on a ranch, even surrounded by friends, left me feeling somewhat isolated and out of touch with the world. I realized that I would be happiest living in a small village, such as Weaver's Flat and Palm Springs. I resolved to tell Mandy how I felt about the matter.

The hours crept by as I waited for Mandy and the others to return. All sunlight was gone, but there was a huge full moon that lit the entire area as brightly as the gas lamps on city streets. I saw the wagon approach from several hundred yards away, followed by the horsemen. I ran out to greet them.

I pulled up short when I reached the wagon. It was not Mandy who was seated next to Albert. It was Carlotta. I took a step back and tried to see the riders on the horses. There were five. To my great relief, one of them was Mandy. She dismounted and wrapped her arm around my waist. It was as much affection as we dared display in public.

She said to the sheriff, "Keep moving, Carl. We'll follow on foot."

When they were out of earshot, she said, "Robert is dead. His body is on the wagon."

Only then did I recognize the horse she rode as Robert's. "I didn't think they intended to kill him. Did something go wrong?"

She nodded. "It started out exactly as planned. Albert and I went to the appointed place. We carried the gold into the cave, which required four trips. Then we sat down to wait. Carlotta appeared from behind us. She had been hiding on the other side of a large boulder inside the cave. She put her index finger to her lips, indicating that we should stay silent."

"Did she have a weapon?" I asked.

"I don't believe so. She examined the gold then went to the mouth of the cave, apparently to send Robert some sort of signal. Albert crept up behind her. He caught a glimpse of Robert in back of a cluster of rocks about a hundred yards away."

"Where his daughter is concerned, Albert tends to make irrational decisions," I said. "I hope he didn't put anyone in danger."

She shook her head. "Unfortunately, he put all of us in danger. He thought if we left the gold and took off with Carlotta in the wagon, Robert would go for the booty and let us escape. He was probably correct in that respect. But Carlotta created a problem. She believed — in fact she *still* believes — that Robert was loyal to her. So when Albert grabbed her and tried to pull her after him toward the wagon, she pulled back. He persisted, and she began to hit his arms in an attempt to free herself." She shrugged. "Apparently it appeared to Robert that his own plan had gone awry in some way that he didn't understand. He fired two shots at Albert."

"The signal to summon the sheriff's men," I said. I began to understand what had happened.

"Precisely. The deputies came around from the back side of the cave immediately. Robert shot at them, but didn't hit anyone. They returned fire and killed him."

"Did Carlotta see it happen?"

She frowned. "Yes, she saw everything. She went quite mad, but not in the way that I would have expected. A bullet hit Robert at his left temple. He was probably dead before he fell to the ground, and everyone knew it. At that point Albert loosened his grip on Carlotta. She lunged at me, screaming that everything was my fault."

I wasn't terribly surprised. "Apparently she still believes that you're to blame for all of her problems."

"So it seems. Albert couldn't pull her away from me, so one of the deputies helped him. She was still screaming and cursing when they lifted her onto the wagon. Someone found Robert's horse and suggested that I ride it back, rather than share the wagon with Carlotta."

At that point, we arrived at the ranch house. "I'm concerned about the prospect of continuing to live in the same house with her," I said.

"I've thought about that. It would be difficult if we were to stay here. I believe it's time to move on."

I was relieved that Mandy felt as she did. Later that night as we lay awake in the dark, I told her my thoughts and feelings about our future.

# Chapter Sixteen

BY MORNING I had not fully recovered from the emotional upheaval of the previous day. Rather than assist with office work, as was my habit, I opted to spend an hour or two in Albert's library. I soon found that I was not alone. At the far end of the room, almost hidden in a cluster of leather-bound chairs, Martha Mae was absorbed in a book.

I decided to select something to read before joining her. I was kneeling, scanning the titles on one of the lower shelves when Mandy entered.

"Is anyone here?" she called.

Behind her, the library door slammed shut. "Yes, as a matter of fact." The rage in Carlotta's voice was terrifying. "I've been waiting for an opportunity to be alone with you."

Mandy sounded calm. "I don't understand why you believe that I was connected to your trouble with Robert."

"You humiliated him," she shouted. "Because of you, everyone believes he tried to hide Irene's divorce papers and her will. Because of you, everyone believes he killed Irene for her money!"

She was too agitated to notice as the door opened softly behind her. Mandy said, "No, Carlotta. On the contrary, there is ample evidence that he could not have killed Irene. Albert has grain contracts from the Sperry Flour Company in San Francisco, signed and dated by Robert on the day she was murdered. He didn't kill her."

"Of course he didn't kill her, you fool! I killed her—just as I'm going to kill you."

When a shot rang out, I jumped up, expecting the worst. But Carlotta's gun had fallen to the floor when it was torn from her hand by a bullet from Martha Mae's derringer.

Carlotta froze for an instant, then lunged for her gun. Martha Mae fired at it once again. *Click*. But in that instant, we had gained the time we needed. Mandy pinned Carlotta's arms to her sides and held on. I kicked the gun in Martha Mae's direction.

Only then did we become aware of Albert's presence. I realized that the soft sound of the door opening a few moments earlier must have been made by him. He walked slowly to the gun on the floor and picked it up.

Carlotta said, "Papa, these women are evil. They killed Irene, and now they intend to kill me."

"No, daughter. I heard what you just said. I saw what you just did. You are the one who is evil. I must summon the sheriff now." Tears ran down his face as he clasped her arm firmly and took her from the room.

Mandy said to Martha Mae, "Thank you for saving my life." She grinned. "By my count, that makes three times."

I made a mental note to ask her later to tell me about the other two times. Martha Mae wasn't listening. She opened her derringer, peered at the dual chambers, and muttered something unintelligible.

"Are both chambers empty?" Mandy asked.

"Yes. I was extremely careless. After that dreadful incident with John Workman, I..." She looked at me. "That is, after...."

I said, "Martha Mae, I shall be eternally grateful to you for saving the life of the woman I love. Therefore, I shall never reveal anything I might learn regarding...uh...people you might have killed."

"Tell us about that second empty chamber," Mandy said. "Is it connected to the murder of Laura's husband?"

She smiled demurely. "It wasn't murder. Technically speaking, it was self-defense. John's plan was to make Laura watch while he killed me. He told her that if she revealed what he had done, he would expose our relationship, and his act would surely be judged as justifiable homicide. Also, he would have her committed to an asylum for the rest of her life."

"From what I've heard of John Workman, that sounds like something he would do with relish," Mandy said.

Martha Mae continued. "He forced her to come with him to the rear of the hotel and call for me to come outside. While he was rambling on about perversion and justice and teaching Laura a lesson, I slipped my derringer from my waistband and shot him to death."

"Didn't the gunshot arouse suspicion?" I asked.

She shrugged. "If it did, nothing came of it. Laura and I dragged his body off the main path, into the shadows. Then I told her to go to your house immediately and to tell you what John had intended to do. When she arrived, she was badly shaken, as you saw. But it wasn't due to the threats John had made. It was because she had just watched him die, and she was frightened that we might be held accountable. So it was imperative that everyone should believe John was still alive. I went into the hotel dining room and came upon James Collier. What better alibi could I have than spending the night with the sheriff?" She chuckled. "He didn't resist."

"After James fell asleep in my bed, I fired his gun out the window and quickly returned it to his holster. I told him I had seen Simon Franklin running away. James ran outside and found John Workman's body. Naturally, he assumed that the gunshot that had awakened him was the one that had killed John. At that point, Simon Franklin became the primary suspect in John's murder."

Mandy said, "It was a good plan. Until it became known that Simon was in jail at the time of the murder, everyone accepted it."

"Yes, it appeared that both Laura and I were above suspicion. She played her role of the grief-stricken widow flawlessly. That was difficult for her. In reality, she was ecstatic to be free of the living hell

John had created." She smiled. "Anyone who gave the matter much thought could have worked out what actually happened. But it was simpler for everyone to accept my explanation."

Not everyone, I thought. I recalled the morning after John's murder, when we were in James Collier's office and Mandy casually examined his gun.

"You knew, didn't you?" I asked her.

"No, I didn't know for certain. But I do know Martha Mae quite well, and I knew in a general way what John would do if he learned of her relationship with Laura." She turned to Martha Mae and said, "As you know, I'm not a believer in coincidence. In view of the circumstances, the situation was too perfect. John Workman was dead, a witness saw Simon Franklin run away from the murder scene, and the sheriff personally discovered the body. I gave the matter some thought."

"Was it that obvious?" Martha Mae asked.

Mandy laughed. "Not at all. I wasn't certain that I had worked it out until I discovered that James's gun had been fired and he didn't seem to be aware of it." She frowned. "But it surprises me that you forgot to reload your derringer."

"It was a serious error. I was counting on that second bullet a few minutes ago," Martha Mae said. "Maybe I'm getting too old for complicated maneuvers such as this. I suppose the time has come to retire from my previous activities."

I said, "I think all of us need to move on. It feels like this place is starting to close in on us."

"Laura has felt that way since shortly after we arrived," Martha Mae said. "We were in such a rush to leave Palm Springs that we didn't have time to consider any other options. We were afraid that someone there would eventually discover the truth about John's death, and we wanted to be out of reach when it occurred. But Laura feels guilty whenever she's in Albert's presence, because I killed his brother and she's happy about it."

Mandy said, "I'm glad we came here. I like this area. But I agree that we don't belong in Albert's home."

Once the topic was open for discussion at last, we expressed our thoughts freely. We all agreed that Albert was a good, kind and honorable man. We also agreed that it was time for all of us to leave the Workman Ranch.


LAURA TOLD ALBERT that she had decided to leave the ranch. She didn't expect him to take the news so badly, but when he explained his feeling about the matter, it made sense to her. His wife was dead. His brother was dead, and he had no other siblings. His only daughter would probably spend most of her life in prison for murder. His only two sons had moved to New York and would probably never return. Laura Workman was the only family member who was still a part of his daily life. Nevertheless, she was shocked when he told her that he wished to give her one thousand acres of his land, the exact location of which was to be determined by her.

She was torn between exuberance and guilt. Fearful of imposing negative or hurtful feelings on Martha Mae, she sought out my opinion on the matter.

"You never harmed John," I told her, "despite the fact that he harmed you a great deal. You have no reason to feel guilty about his death or about accepting Albert's gift."

She began to weep. "I've never regretted what happened. But I don't see how I can bring myself to profit from it."

"Albert and John grew up together. Albert is no fool. He knew his brother, and surely he knows what your life with John must have been like. He wants to do this for you. Don't refuse him."

She stopped crying and looked at me. "I've never thought of it that way. Yes, I see it."

After she composed herself, we discussed where one might wish to own a thousand acres in the San Fernando Valley. The new railroad seemed to act as a magnet for settlers and possible land development. If Albert was amenable, Laura would ask him for the thousand acres of the ranch that were adjacent to the proposed Chatsworth Park Railroad Station.


ALBERT PRAISED LAURA for her intelligent decision and initiated the paperwork to transfer title for the designated property to her. In less than a week, the land was hers.

She sold us five acres at the going rate of one dollar per acre. Shortly thereafter, we commissioned a modest one-story house to be built at the exact center of the parcel.

Laura and Martha Mae opted for a more lavish appearance. Their new home was to be a large two-story redwood structure. Martha Mae left all of the planning to Laura, with the exception of the library. Now that she was retired from her former line of work, she was determined to tap some of the fortune that Jakey had given her from the Lost Dutchman Mine and to focus her efforts on creating the finest private library in California.


A FEW MILES north of our newly procured property was a farmhouse that had been vacant for several years. The owners had retired and moved closer to the center of Los Angeles to live with their son, who had established a successful hardware business. Although they did not want to sell their land, they were happy to rent the house to us while we awaited completion of our new homes. It was barely large enough for the four of us, but we were grateful for a refuge from the uncomfortable atmosphere that had settled over the Workman Ranch.

We completed our move from the ranch in less than a day. Since we had no furniture or other large items, we were able to bring everything we owned in a wagon that Albert had given us. Only when we brought our possessions into the house did I realize the horrible condition it was in. Fortunately, the owners had left behind enough furniture to meet our immediate needs. After several days of cleaning and removing trash, we began to feel comfortable.

About twenty yards from the rear of the house were the remains of a vegetable garden that had been neglected for a few years. Someone had once put a great deal of work into getting it established, and I felt that I could make it productive with a relatively small effort.

I found a spade in the barn and set to work turning the soil and removing the weeds. All went well until I turned over what appeared to be the remains of a human foot.

"Mandy!" My legs gave out. Suddenly I was seated on the ground.

I stared in horror at the foot. I heard Mandy rush up behind me and come to an abrupt halt. She squatted beside me, looked at the foot, and cocked her head.

"Hmm."

"I...I think we need to notify someone," I said shakily.

"Yes." She stood up. "I'll go for Sheriff Jacobsen. Don't touch anything here."

She was several steps away before she noticed that I had not moved. She came back and helped me to my feet.

Her tone was gentle. "I'm sorry, sweetheart. I didn't stop to think that this would be so upsetting to you. Sometimes I forget that you and I come from different backgrounds."

She put her arm around my waist and walked me to the house. Then she saddled Daisy and set out to find Carl Jacobsen.


THE THREE HOURS that Mandy was gone seemed like an eternity. I alternately paced the floor and squinted out the front window for some sign of her. At last she returned with Carl and one of his deputies.

They examined the area cautiously. They dug a shallow trough about two feet wide all the way around the body. The flesh was completely gone. The only remnants of clothing were a partially decomposed leather belt, a belt buckle and a few metal buttons. They sifted carefully through the dirt as they removed it. They found several coins, the newest of which was a one-cent piece bearing the date 1881.

After about an hour, Doc Halverson arrived, having been summoned in his capacity as coroner. He examined the remains.

He was a man of few words. "Male. Old — at least fifty. Shattered skull — looks like a gunshot to the head at close range. I'll send the wagon to pick him up tomorrow." He turned and left without another word.

Before Carl and his deputy left, Mandy found an old canvas tarp in the barn that they used to cover the body. As I watched their departure, my thoughts turned to the man in the shallow grave. The possibility that his identity would ever be known was slim.

The wagon from the Coroner's Office arrived the next day, and two men carried away the remains. There was an obvious dip in the ground where the body had been. I abandoned my plans for the vegetable garden.

We spent the next months monitoring the progress in construction of our new houses. Laura was obsessed with her kitchen. Martha Mae scoured newspapers from the East in search of rare books for sale, and began to purchase them. Everyone seemed to have forgotten the incident of the corpse in the backyard.

# Chapter Seventeen

THE DAY OUR new house was ready for occupancy was one of the happiest of my life. We had purchased most of our furnishings by mail from the East, and they had been brought by railroad and stored at the Workman Ranch in the same wooden crates they had been shipped in. Albert sent two wagons—one for Mandy and me, the other for Laura and Martha Mae—to transfer everything we had accumulated to the appropriate location. Daisy and the mule settled into their new quarters with no fuss.

Several dozen people were invited to our housewarming. It was an eclectic mix of some of the local ranchers and farmers, along with many of Albert's employees. In order to ensure that no individual was inadvertently overlooked, we issued an invitation to "the entire staff of the Workman Ranch." One result was that we were decidedly not fond of some of our guests. In particular, we were not pleased to see Hazel Moran, the upstairs housekeeper who had made no secret of her vehement disapproval of us, and Peter Blaylock, Albert's head accountant who had gone to great lengths to keep his activities hidden and thus made our efforts to work in the office more difficult than they might otherwise have been.

WE ESTABLISHED A new living pattern. Without intending to, I found gainful employment as a schoolteacher. The rapid influx of English speaking settlers into the San Fernando Valley resulted in a shortage of English speaking teachers for their children. When Albert made it known that I had experience in teaching, they sought me out. Once again, I was spending my days doing the work I liked best.

Mandy bought a typewriter. She began to write news reports and editorials about local events, and to send them to the Los Angeles Times under the name M. T. Wells. The editor liked her work, published most of it, and hired her to write a weekly editorial column.

Meanwhile, construction began at the Chatsworth Park Railroad Station. One day a man from the Western Union Company arrived to oversee the establishment of a telegraph office within the station. When Mandy learned of this, she made his acquaintance as quickly as possible. His name was Ben Turnquist, and his employer had given him the task of opening and staffing the office. Considering himself extremely fortunate to find a trained telegraph operator, he hired Mandy immediately. Telegraph service was made available on weekdays, either in the morning or the afternoon, to accommodate the passenger trains to and from San Francisco. Local residents arranged their requirements for the service to fit the schedule.

Laura remained loyal to Albert. She spent two or three days of each week in the offices at the Workman Ranch. At Albert's insistence, the reluctant and uncooperative Peter Blaylock allowed her access to some of the accounting ledgers. She used the remainder of her time to improve her house and cultivate a vegetable garden. Martha Mae continued to amass dozens of books for her library. According to Laura, the work did not proceed as quickly as it might have. Martha Mae cataloged each new acquisition and designated a place for it on the shelves. But then progress came to a temporary halt because she simply could not resist reading it cover-to-cover.

We made the naïve assumption that our idyllic life would continue indefinitely, or maybe we simply refused to think of the future. Whatever we might have imagined, it was not what occurred. Less than six months after we moved into our new home, one of Albert's employees was found stabbed to death.


THE NEW RAILROAD station had quickly become an informal gathering place. Every morning, Sheriff Carl Jacobsen was among those who could be found in the small diner in the rear of the building, adjacent to the telegraph office. On the day the body of the murdered man was discovered, Sheriff Jacobsen was among a group of men drinking coffee in the diner.

"Jasper Ketchum arrived at the station in a panic," Mandy said. "He ran toward the diner shouting "Sheriff, murder, Sheriff, murder, Sheriff, murder" all the way across the lobby."

Jasper Ketchum was prone to exaggeration. "Was there actually a murder?" I asked.

"Yes. But I didn't learn the details until later. Jasper said a stabbing had occurred out at Clara Bowen's farm. Carl left right away to investigate. At the exact minute the telegraph office was scheduled to close, I locked up and headed out to the Bowen place."

Clara Bowen was a widow whose husband Jared had succumbed to tuberculosis ten years earlier. Jared's father Andrew owned the farm. Andrew Bowen was a disagreeable man who did not approve of his son's wife. Before Jared's death, it was common knowledge that he would inherit the farm from his father. With Jared gone, however, Clara's future was uncertain. The farm was profitable enough that she could afford to pay a man to operate it and earn a reasonable income for herself. Absent any communication from Andrew Bowen, she carried on with her life.

Mandy said, "When I arrived, Clara was almost in a state of nervous collapse. I assured her that I would have Doc Halverson come out there. She needed some sort of concoction to settle her down."

"Medication. Not concoction," I said.

She nodded. "Medication. She was in the parlor, collapsed into a big chair. Carl Jacobsen tried simultaneously to calm her down and to get her to tell him what had happened. It did not go well."

"Was she finally able to tell you who was murdered?"

"She didn't have to. It was Albert's accountant, Peter Blaylock. His body was in the foyer, just inside the front door."

To my knowledge, there was no connection between Peter Blaylock and Clara Bowen. In fact, the disgusting little man generally kept to himself in his bungalow on the Workman Ranch. During the time we lived at the ranch, I had always avoided him at midday dinner.

"Why do you suppose Peter went to the Bowen farm?" I asked.

"Clara claims it was to rob her. When she caught him in the act, he tried to strangle her. She managed to secure a knife, and in the scuffle that followed, she killed him."

"I don't understand this. Peter made a good salary. He didn't need to rob anyone...least of all an old widow. Moreover, if he wanted money, don't you think it would have been easier for him to embezzle it from Albert?"

Mandy said, "I've often wondered why Peter was so secretive about his work. Laura mentioned it several times while she was doing bookkeeping chores for Albert. If he was embezzling Albert's money, that would explain his behavior."

"But it wouldn't explain his presence in Clara's house," I said.

"There was something else I couldn't explain at Clara's. There was a pool of blood under Peter's body, and no blood anywhere else. The knife that killed him was still there, covered with blood."

I said, "Obviously the struggle was confined to the foyer."

"I went into the kitchen and found more knives. The knife that killed Peter was one of a set. Three other identical knives were neatly lined up in a drawer." She frowned. "If Clara discovered Peter in the foyer of her house, she would have asked him what he was doing there. She would not simply decide to kill him for no reason."

"Perhaps she had a reason," I said.

"Perhaps. It appears that she went to the kitchen, took a knife from the drawer, and returned to the foyer, and all the while Peter did nothing either to stop her or to try to escape."

"That makes no sense," I said.

"Most of this story makes no sense. I intend to give the matter some serious thought."

"Are you going to write a newspaper report about this?" I asked.

"Yes." She winked at me. "Under the circumstances, it will be completely free of useful information."

```
Man Found Stabbed to Death
Special Report to the Times by M. T. Wells

Mr. Peter Blaylock, formerly of Chicago and most
```

recently head accountant at the Workman Ranch in the
San Fernando Valley, died on Thursday, July 5, at the
home of Mrs. Clara Bowen. According to Sheriff Carl
Jacobsen, the incident involved foul play that
culminated with the stabbing death of Mr. Blaylock.
The associated investigation is ongoing. Interested
parties are advised to contact the Halverson Mortuary
for information on burial arrangements.

Because he had trusted Peter Blaylock without reservation in all of
his business transactions, Albert was particularly distraught. In his
view, since his accountant had been accused of attempted burglary, the
integrity of his entire operation had been called into question. The
prestigious Los Angeles accounting firm of Crandall and Smith
performed an in-depth audit of his books. Herbert Crandall III
personally reported that the books were in perfect order.

Albert asked Laura to supervise the examination and removal of
Peter's personal property from the bungalow he had occupied on the
ranch. Laura in turn asked me to assist her. We began the following
afternoon. We were joined by Ruth Canfield, an old friend of Albert's
deceased wife and a longtime resident of the area.

Most of the furnishings were ranch property. They would be left for
the next occupant. Clothing, shoes, books, stationery and anything else
that was usable would be donated to local churches. Personal items
such as photographs and letters would be boxed and kept permanently
in a small storage area at the rear of Albert's library.

I felt like an unwelcome intruder as I sifted through Peter's desk
drawers. Most of the contents were what I termed "desk junk" — a
battered pair of scissors, a scarred wooden ruler, pieces of string and
wire of various lengths and more than a dozen pencils that needed to be
sharpened. I put all of it into a small canvas bag that I would take to
school. Whatever my students did not want would become trash.

The only thing in the desk of a personal nature was an elaborately
carved wooden box. Inside were three items that seemed unrelated. The
first was a worn sepia photograph of a man who was unknown to me.
He wore a checked shirt and dark trousers. I was unable to estimate his
age, but I could tell that he was not a young man.

The second item was an old newspaper clipping. It said that Mr.
Dexter Bowen, brother of deceased local resident Jared Bowen, had
arrived recently to visit and offer comfort to Jared's widow. He planned
to stay for a month before returning to his home in Ohio. I stared at the
clipping for several minutes. It was the link we sought between Peter
Blaylock and Clara Bowen, but its significance was unclear to me.

The third item was a bankbook. It contained monthly entries dating
back nearly five years in amounts varying from nine to fifteen dollars.
The name of the account holder was shown at the top of the first page.

"Sunset Grain Transport," I murmured.

I didn't realize that I had spoken aloud until Laura asked, "What did you say?"

"Sunset Grain Transport. Have you heard of it?"

She nodded. "I've seen cheques issued by the Workman Ranch to that company. There's never been anything remarkable about any of them."

"Did Albert issue the cheques?" I asked.

"No, Peter Blaylock wrote out the details on all the cheques issued by the Workman Ranch, and..." her eyes widened. "...Albert merely signed them! Since he trusted Peter without reservation, he didn't examine the names of the payees or the sums paid."

"Peter must have established a business called Sunset Grain Transport for the sole purpose of embezzling money from the ranch," I said.

Laura picked up the bankbook and perused the entries. "When Crandall and Smith audited Albert's books, it's no wonder that this escaped their notice. All of the cheques were in reasonable amounts, signed by Albert, and properly recorded in the appropriate ledgers."

During the short walk from Peter's bungalow to the main house, Laura explained their accounting procedures to me. With his unlimited access to all financial transactions, it was easy to understand how Peter could have deceived his trusting employer.

We entered the office that Peter had occupied, and Laura retrieved the cheque ledger. She noted the most recent date in the bankbook and ran her finger down the ledger until she found the corresponding date and Sunset Grain Transport listed as payee.

She frowned. "There's an error."

"What sort of error?"

"According to the ledger, the amount of the cheque was eight dollars and fifty-two cents. But the bankbook shows a deposit of ten dollars and fifty-two cents."

"What does the next entry show?"

She repeated the procedure. "The same error occurred a month earlier. The cheque amount was seven dollars and eighty-six cents, but the bank recorded a deposit of nine dollars and eighty-six cents." She looked up at me. "What an odd coincidence."

I thought of Mandy's observations in past situations. "I'm not a big believer in coincidence," I said.

We verified that the two-dollar discrepancy occurred for every deposit. Then we retrieved the canceled cheques and verified that the amounts matched the ledger entries.


THAT EVENING I related our findings to Mandy. She was fascinated by the puzzle of the two-dollar discrepancy.

"Where is the account? I mean, which bank has it?"

"The Sunset Grain Transport account is with Farmers and Merchants' Bank. I don't know if he had a personal account. We didn't find any evidence of one."

Mandy said, "Peter had a bankbook in his wallet when he was killed. I examined it. His personal account was with First National Bank. There were no suspicious deposits. His salary was four dollars per month. He had accumulated a balance of just over eleven dollars."

I said, "It would have been almost impossible for him to have saved two dollars from his salary every month. The unexplained money that was deposited to the Sunset Grain Transport account must have come from a different source."

She nodded. "And if we can identify that source, it might explain the discrepancy."

# Chapter Eighteen

MANDY WAS PENSIVE the next evening. Rather than reading, as was her habit, she sat perfectly still, deep in thought, and gazed at the flames in the fireplace. I sat in my chair and waited. I had learned from experience that it was fruitless to interrupt her concentration.

Finally she said, "Laura came to the railroad station today."

"She mentioned that she hasn't seen you recently. It was nice of her to visit."

"She didn't come to see me. She was looking for Carl. She brought Peter Blaylock's wooden box...the one you told me about."

"Including the contents?"

"Yes, even the bankbook. She said that Albert thinks all of it could be evidence of something more sinister than simply stealing his money."

I said, "On that we all agree. The question is, where do we go from here?"

"Carl showed that old photograph to the men at the diner. Nobody recognized the man in it. Charlie Gilbert said he thought it looked like a smaller, thinner version of Jared Bowen, but the others disagreed." She shrugged. "As I understand it, Jared Bowen has been dead for several years. Most of those men probably don't recall what he looked like, or they never even met him."

"But Charlie may have hit upon something," I said. "That old newspaper clipping mentioned the Bowens. There must be a connection."

"Did you happen to notice the belt the man in the photograph was wearing?" she asked.

I shook my head. "I concentrated on the face. But the image is so small and blurry, I couldn't make it out. I didn't pay much attention to the rest."

She turned back to the fire. "There are so many unanswered questions. We need to dig deeper."


THE NEXT EVENING was much the same. Mandy stared silently at the fire, lost in thought. I waited.

At last she said, "Carl and I went to Los Angeles this morning. We visited Farmers and Merchants' Bank."

"How did you convince him to let you accompany him?"

She smiled. "Actually, the trip was my idea. I told him I was working on a report of Peter Blaylock's murder for the Times, and I had obtained a critical piece of information that I needed to verify. When he asked about the details, I insisted that it would make sense only after the people at the bank provided the missing pieces to the puzzle. He couldn't resist accompanying me."

"What information had you obtained?"

"Frankly, I had nothing. But I was certain that I needed to have Carl with me at the bank. I wanted to learn whatever facts they might be able to provide regarding Peter and Sunset Grain Transport." A piece of kindling snapped and a spark flew out of the fireplace. She kicked it back. "I felt that even if they weren't inclined to be forthcoming with me, they would surely cooperate with a law enforcement officer. As it turned out, I was correct."

"Did you learn anything of value?" I asked.

"Possibly. At first, the bank teller we spoke with was rude and unhelpful. Regardless of what question we asked, his response was that he was not at liberty to provide that information. Finally Carl demanded that we speak with someone in authority. After a considerable delay, we ended up in the vice president's office. He knew nothing of the matter, so he summoned the same teller we had dealt with earlier. It was a miraculous transformation," she said with a laugh. "In his employer's presence, the man was pleasant and cooperative."

"What did he tell you?"

"Peter came to the bank only once each month to make a deposit, which invariably consisted of two dollars in cash and one or two cheques issued by the Workman Ranch. He never made a withdrawal."

"Was the bank able to provide any information about Sunset Grain Transport?" I asked.

She nodded. "On the form Peter submitted when he opened the account, he listed himself as the sole owner. And here's the part that I haven't worked out: the address he listed is that of Clara Bowen."

"The unexplained connection has appeared once again," I said as I rose from my chair. "I think we need to think deeply on this. Perhaps if we were to go to bed, an idea might occur to us."

She jumped up and grinned. "In fact, an idea has just now occurred to me."

She pressed her body into mine and kissed me deeply. She touched me in all the right places, and within moments I was on fire with my need for her. Talk of Peter Blaylock and everything related to him was finished for the night.


THE FOLLOWING AFTERNOON, I was detained at the school after my class was dismissed for the day. One of my students, Archie Ketchum, had a habit of wandering off into neighboring fields and pastures, sometimes dallying far into the night, whenever he was left on his own. Because of this, he was never to leave my sight until I turned him over to his older brother, Jasper. Unfortunately, Jasper was late.

At twelve years of age, Archie had the reading skill of a seven-year-old. Like the rest of the Ketchum family, he was termed mentally "slow," but was not considered retarded. I was confident that the Ketchum children would find a way to enjoy independent and happy lives.

As I awaited his arrival, I recalled that it was Jasper who had reported Peter Blaylock's murder to the sheriff. To my knowledge, nobody had asked him how he knew about it or what he had seen.

At last he burst into the classroom. "Sorry to be late, Miss Reynolds. I was delayed."

"That's all right, Jasper. Would you take a seat please? I'd like to ask you some questions."

An expression of panic came over his face. "Am I in trouble?"

"No, not at all. I'd like for you to tell me about how you happened to be out at the Bowen farm on the day Peter Blaylock died, and I'd like to know what you saw there."

He took a seat at a desk in the front row. "My Ma mended some clothes for Mrs. Bowen. She sent me out there to deliver 'em." He frowned. "I was supposed to collect five cents, but I never did. I got confused when I saw Mr. Blaylock and all that blood. That's when I ran away."

"Where was Mr. Blaylock's body?"

"Right by the front door. The door was open, and he was just inside, on the floor." His eyes widened. "There was so much blood!"

"And Mrs. Bowen, did you see her?"

He nodded. "She was right there on her knees, kind of tugging and jerking at Mr. Blaylock. Then she looked up at me, and her eyes reminded me of an angry bull. She shouted, 'Oh, no!' She scared me. I turned around and ran until I got to the railroad station. I knew Sheriff Jacobsen would be there."

He grew increasingly upset as he talked. It appeared that little would be gained by pressing him further.

I said, "Thank you for telling me what happened, Jasper."

"Can I go now, Miss Reynolds?"

"Yes, Jasper."

During our exchange, young Archie Ketchum had been lost in a dream world as he studied the illustrations in a book about exotic birds. Jasper removed the book from his hands and handed it to me. Then he took Archie's hand and left the room in great haste.

I TOLD MANDY about Jasper's experience at the Bowen farm. As I expected, she proceeded to analyze each detail.

"Clara Bowen's reaction is odd," she said. "If you had just killed a man who was trying to rob you, and then Jasper appeared, what would you say?"

I imagined myself in the situation she described. "I would tell him to get the sheriff."

"I believe most people would say that. Most people would be relieved if Jasper had appeared at that point. But Clara said, 'oh, no,' which indicates that she didn't want him there."

"He told me her eyes were as angry as a bull's," I said.

She nodded. "If Jasper's presence made her angry, he must have interrupted her while she was doing something she wanted to keep secret."

I said, "I don't know how she could have kept Peter's death a secret. Even though she's a sturdy little woman and he probably didn't weigh much more than a hundred and sixty pounds, his body was too heavy for her to move. She could not possibly have disposed of it without...segmenting it first. And she didn't have enough time for that. Her hired help would have discovered her before she could finish and clean up the horrible evidence."

"You've forgotten your lessons in physics. Do you remember how we gained access to Jakey's mine?"

Leverage. With a few long pieces of wood, Clara could move Peter's body several feet in a short time. I had seen Mandy use the same principle to move the boulders that covered the entrance to the Lost Dutchman Mine.

I nodded. "I understand how she could have moved the body. But I'm not clear as to why she would want to do it."

"Back up, April. If you were on a farm, and you wanted to hide a body where it wasn't likely to be found, and you had very little time to do it, how would you proceed?"

After a moment's thought I said, "I would find a place where the soil was relatively loose and dig a grave...I suppose it would be quite shallow. Then I would use a few shovel handles as levers to transfer the body into the grave. After that, I would need only a few minutes to cover it over and clean up. I could complete the entire task in less than two hours."

Mandy snapped her fingers. "The vegetable garden. Clara has an extensive vegetable garden."

Suddenly an unwelcome memory came to mind. I thought of the vegetable garden behind the house we rented while awaiting completion of our new home. I thought of the man whose remains were buried there in a shallow grave. Other than his skeleton, the only evidence of his existence was stored in a small box at the Sheriff's Office: a few coins, six metal buttons and a belt buckle.

I was overcome by a wave of sadness. "Coins, buttons and a belt buckle," I murmured.

"What did you say?"

"I was thinking of the man whose remains were buried in the vegetable garden in back of the house we used to rent."

She stared at me. "He was shot in the head and...I wonder if Clara...." She jumped up. "I want to speak with the people who own that house."

The name of our former landlord was listed in my address book. He and his wife lived over their son's hardware store on Fourth Street near South Broadway in Los Angeles. Mandy planned to call on them the next morning.

Since it was Saturday and the school was closed, I was able to accompany Mandy. We went first to the sheriff's office.

Carl Jacobsen was reluctant to loan us the photograph that had been found in Peter Blaylock's desk. He explained that it was a violation of protocol. He fretted that we might lose it, and there would be serious repercussions. He pondered the possibility of accompanying us, although it would mean forgoing a barbecue at the Dreyer ranch. Finally, he retrieved the photograph and turned it over to Mandy. We continued on our way.


MARK ANDERSON, JR. owned and operated the highly successful Anderson Hardware and Supply. He lived nearby with his wife and three children in a two-story Victorian house that reflected his prosperity. His parents, Mark Sr. and Judith, lived above the hardware store in a comfortable apartment.

Although we had once rented their house, our dealings with the Andersons had been conducted entirely by mail. Mark Jr. led us upstairs and introduced us to his parents. They looked like a matched set. Both had silver-gray hair. Both wore wire-rimmed spectacles, well-worn oversized cardigan sweaters and house slippers.

They were curious about us. Only after we answered their questions regarding our current residence and activities would they permit the conversation to proceed to other matters. Mandy showed them the photograph. The man looked familiar, but....

"When was this taken?" Judith Anderson asked.

Mandy said, "Probably about ten years ago. Maybe a little longer."

Judith handed the photograph to her husband. "Mark, this reminds me a little of that man from Indiana...the one who rented the house shortly after we moved out of it."

"No, it was Ohio. I recall it quite clearly." He handed it back. "His name was Bowers...Bowden...something like that."

"No, it was Bowen," she said. "I recall it clearly now." She turned to Mandy. "Mr. Bowen. His given name was Delbert, I believe."

Mark said, "No, it was Dexter. That's it. Dexter Bowen from Ohio. He stayed in the house for a couple of months, paid his rent on time, then suddenly he was gone."

"Do you mean that he returned to Ohio?" Mandy asked.

He shrugged. "I don't know what happened to him. When my son went to the house to collect the rent for the forthcoming month, nobody was there. That is, nobody was living there. The house was clean and there were no personal items in it, so we just assumed that he'd left."

Judith said, "Since he didn't owe any back rent, we didn't pursue it. Two months later we found another tenant." She looked at Mark. "I don't believe we ever thought about Mr. Bowen after that."

"No, I don't believe so," he replied.

We thanked the Andersons for their hospitality. Together they escorted us down the stairs and left us at the rear of the hardware store. As we made our way through the store to the front door, we came upon their son.

"Were my parents able to help you?" he asked.

I said, "Yes, between them they had all the information we sought."

"They work as a team," he said with a twinkle in his eyes.

"And a very good team, at that," I said.


WHEN WE WERE out of earshot Mandy said, "Have you looked closely at that photograph lately?"

"No. It doesn't hold much meaning for me, since I never met Dexter Bowen."

"I don't mean the man or his face. Look at the belt buckle he was wearing."

I pulled the photograph from its envelope in my handbag. The image was fuzzy. I said, "I can barely make it out. It looks like it may be gold or brass colored...maybe in the shape of a figure eight...I can't be certain."

"Do you recall the belt buckle we found in the Andersons' vegetable garden?"

I shuddered at the memory. "I don't believe I could ever forget it." Then my heart stopped as the realization sank in. "They could be the same. The remains could be those of Dexter Bowen!"

"We can verify it with at the sheriff's office," she said.

We arrived less than an hour later. At first Carl didn't understand why we wanted to compare evidence from two different cases. But when we set the belt buckle next to the photograph, the answer was obvious.


AS WE SET out for home Mandy said, "What facts do we know about this?"

Once again, I tried to put my thoughts in order. "One: Dexter Bowen was in the San Fernando Valley either shortly before or shortly after his brother Jared died of tuberculosis."

"We can safely assume that," she said.

"Two: Dexter was killed by a gunshot to the head and buried in the vegetable garden behind the house where he was living."

She nodded. "Indisputable."

"Three: Peter Blaylock had a photograph of Dexter in his desk."

"Also true."

"Four: Clara Bowen stabbed Peter Blaylock to death when she caught him in the act of burglarizing her home."

She shook her head. "I agree that Clara killed Peter. But we have no proof that it was self-defense. It doesn't make sense that he went to her house to burglarize it. In fact, considering his other activities, I would rule out burglary entirely." She frowned. "We still need to dig deeper."

# Chapter Nineteen

TO MY SURPRISE, Mandy convinced Carl Jacobsen that we could extract the truth from Clara Bowen. We didn't have a clear idea of what we wanted from Clara. The plan in general was to ask nebulous questions and listen for specific answers. I was not optimistic.

Carl, Mandy and I went to the Bowen farm at midmorning. Clara answered Carl's knock at the front door and invited us to join her for coffee. Since it was Sunday, her hired hand was absent, so we had Clara's undivided attention. We followed her to the kitchen and took seats at a round table that was covered with a faded red and white checked tablecloth. Clara set out four mugs of steaming coffee.

"We're here to ask you some questions about Peter Blaylock," Carl said.

She looked at Mandy, then back at Carl. "Might I ask why these...uh...ladies have accompanied you?" Her voice dripped with sarcasm when she uttered the word "ladies."

I glanced at Mandy. Having heard countless remarks about her habit of dressing in buckskin trousers and flannel shirts, she was undisturbed by Clara's gibe.

"They have questions for you, as well," he said. "I convinced them to accompany me so that they might speak with you directly. But first I want to ask you about Peter. Did you know him personally?"

She shook her head. "I knew him by sight, and I suppose he knew who I was, but we were never formally introduced."

"What did you know about him?"

"Only that he was Albert Workman's accountant."

Carl retrieved the photograph of Dexter Bowen and placed it on the table. "Do you know this man?"

She drew a sharp breath, then composed herself quickly. "I don't believe so."

"Look closely, Mrs. Bowen. Is it your brother-in-law, Dexter?"

A flash of panic in her eyes disappeared after a fraction of a second. "Oh...yes, I suppose it could be him."

Carl pressed on. "Dexter was murdered several years ago, not far from here."

"I wasn't aware of that." She clutched the apron in her lap.

"I'm surprised you didn't know, considering the fact that he came here to visit you."

She began to twist the apron fabric. "He did visit me. Then he left. I haven't seen him since."

It was evident to me that Clara Bowen intended to deny any connection to the death of her brother-in-law. I decided to take a gamble.

"You killed Dexter Bowen," I said.

She looked at me, wide-eyed. "That's impossible! I don't even own a gun."

Had Carl mentioned that Dexter Bowen was killed by a gunshot? I couldn't recall.

I continued with my ploy. "We know that you killed him. We don't know why you did it, but we can find out. Perhaps if you were to cooperate with Sheriff Jacobsen by providing him with the facts he seeks..." I shrugged.

Mandy took up the pursuit. "Mrs. Bowen, don't you find it a curious coincidence that this photograph of Dexter was in Peter Blaylock's desk? I wonder if its purpose was to serve as a reminder to him...or to someone."

"I don't know anything about that. It has nothing to do with me."

Mandy said, "Peter was not an honorable man. We've uncovered evidence that he committed serious crimes. But his crimes were never of a physical nature. That is, he didn't rob banks or burglarize houses."

"He came into my house to steal things." Her tone was both frightened and angry.

Mandy leaned toward her. "That isn't why he was here, Mrs. Bowen. He came as he did every month, to collect two dollars in cash from you. Over the course of ten years, two dollars per month adds up to a considerable sum."

"No!"

Mandy took a bigger gamble than I had. "We have proof. Perhaps you were pushed beyond your limits."

Clara Bowen gave up. She dissolved before our eyes. Her defiant tone became soft and resigned. "Dexter didn't deserve to die. He was my father-in-law's pawn, just as my husband was." A tear appeared in her eye, and she wiped it away. "Andrew Bowen hated me from the day he met me. I have no idea why. When Jared married me, Andrew swore that I would never profit from his family's wealth."

"Was Andrew Bowen a wealthy man?" Mandy asked.

She shook her head. "Not particularly. But he was obsessed with controlling his sons' lives. He gave Jared the farm, but retained title to the land. There was an understanding that Jared would inherit it eventually." She took a deep breath. "Less than a month after my husband died, Andrew decided to evict me from the farm. He sent Dexter, his surviving son, to ensure that I vacated the premises and left everything behind. Dexter didn't want to do it. But he was terrified of his father, so he dared not disobey his orders."

Her eyes reflected the grief and remorse she had borne alone for ten years. Having begun the story, she appeared eager to complete it and thus unburden herself of her dreadful secret.

She turned to Carl. "One evening I brought a horse and wagon to the house that Dexter was living in while he worked at the task his father had given him." She glanced at Mandy. "It was the same house you rented before your permanent home here was completed." She looked back at Carl. "I brought Jared's pistol. Dexter invited me to join him for coffee at the kitchen table. When he turned to the stove to make a pot of coffee, I shot him in the back of the head."

I jerked back involuntarily. Although I knew the truth, it was a shock to hear her confess it. She took another deep breath. She had more to tell.

"I found a few long pieces of scrap lumber in the barn. I used them as levers to move Dexter's body out to the old vegetable garden, where the soil was soft. I dug a hole about two feet deep and pushed him in. Then I said a prayer for him and covered him over." She leaned back and gazed at the ceiling. "I loaded all of his possessions onto my wagon, cleaned up his house, and went home." She pressed the palm of her hand against her forehead. "I thought...I don't know...I suppose I thought that with Dexter gone, it would be the end of my trouble with Andrew."

Mandy said, "But there was trouble with someone else, wasn't there?"

Tears rolled down her face. "Yes. It was Peter Blaylock. I don't know the extent of his involvement in the matter, but he knew everything." Once again she began to twist the apron fabric in her lap. "He said that as long as I gave him a dollar every month, he would keep my secret. I paid him for a year. Then he increased the amount to two dollars. I've paid Peter all this time. And I've paid the County property taxes on that land all this time, even though Andrew Bowen is still the owner of record. There's never been anyone else to challenge my presence on the farm."

"Tell us about how you...about how Peter Blaylock died," Carl said.

"It happened when he came here to collect his monthly fee. As usual, he waited in the foyer for me to get the money from the metal box that I keep in the kitchen." She closed her eyes. "As I reached into the box, a compelling thought occurred to me. I realized that if Peter were to disappear, I would be free of his threats and blackmail forever."

"By 'disappear' do you mean 'cease to live'?" Carl asked.

She opened her eyes. "Yes. So rather than take the money from my metal box, I took a knife from my top drawer. I returned to the foyer. Peter didn't look at me when he held out his hand for the money. He was frowning at his wristwatch. He never even saw the knife."

Upon hearing my sharp intake of breath, she looked at me and said, "On a farm one learns to kill quickly and humanely."

"That was the point at which Jasper Ketchum appeared," Mandy said.

She nodded. "Peter had opened the front door just before he died. Jasper appeared about three minutes later to deliver some clothing that his mother had mended for me. By then the blood had begun to accumulate on the floor of the foyer."

"That ended your plan to dispose of the body," Mandy said.

"Yes. I had planned to bury Peter in the same way I buried Dexter. Then I was going to turn his horse loose. She could find her way home easily. By the time she arrived at the Workman Ranch, I would have eliminated all traces of Peter."

Carl said, "But Jasper Ketchum changed all that."

"When I saw Jasper, I was shocked. I cried out, 'Oh, no.' He threw down the mended clothing he had brought and ran away so quickly that I couldn't catch him. I realized that my plan was ruined."

"And you were left with the rather implausible story that Peter was a burglar," I said.

Clara said, "It was the only remaining alternative. Unfortunately, it aroused a great deal of curiosity."

Carl rose from his chair. "You'll have to come with me now, Mrs. Bowen."

> Local Woman Arrested for Double Homicide
> Special Report to the Times by M. T. Wells
>
> Mrs. Clara Bowen was arrested on June 26 for the murder of Peter Blaylock, head accountant at the Workman Ranch. According to Sheriff Carl Jacobsen, Mr. Blaylock was engaged for several years in a ruthless blackmail operation, as well as an elaborate scheme to embezzle significant amounts of money from his employer. According to Albert Workman, owner of the Workman Ranch, the total amount that Blaylock stole from him has not yet been determined.
>
> Mrs. Bowen was also arrested for the 1884 murder of Dexter Bowen of Ohio. Sources close to the investigation say that Dexter Bowen came to the San Fernando Valley shortly after the death of Mrs. Bowen's husband Jared in order to intimidate her to surrender her farm to the Bowen family.
>
> Further details will be reported as the investigation continues.

"Is it possible that your report of the Bowen Blaylock matter is just a bit biased?" I asked.

Mandy's eyes widened. "Of course not! Every word in the article is the absolute objective truth."

# Chapter Twenty

AFTER THE TRAUMATIC experience with Clara Bowen, I was relieved to return to my daily routine of teaching. Like the population of the San Fernando Valley, the size of my class was increasing rapidly. I wondered when the influx of people would end.

For reasons I could not fathom, Mandy took a liking to Clara Bowen. She assured Clara that she would supervise the operation of her farm during the liquidation of its assets. Most of the animals were sold within a month. Hardware and equipment were next. All proceeds of the sales were earmarked for Clara's legal expenses.

Laura and Martha Mae listened with interest as I related the story of Clara's actions. When I finished, Martha Mae shrugged and excused herself to return to her library. Laura, however, wanted additional information. In particular, she was interested in whatever I could tell her about Peter Blaylock.

Laura told me that upon learning of Blaylock's accounting scam, Albert Workman feared that it was just the tip of an iceberg. He enlisted her to complete a thorough examination of revenues and expenditures for the Workman Ranch over the past ten years.

"That's a monumental task for only one person," I said.

Laura said, "In light of what happened, Albert doesn't trust anyone outside of his family. With both of his sons in New York, I'm the only one left."

She did not mention Carlotta. Following the disgrace she had brought upon the Workman family, nobody ever mentioned Carlotta.


OUR LIVES PROCEEDED without incident for two months. Then the illusion of normalcy began to unravel one day when Laura asked for my assistance with her accounting task. It was mid-afternoon when I locked my classroom and went to the Workman Ranch. Laura showed me her predicament.

"I've come upon a few expenditures that concern me," she said.

"In what way do they concern you?"

She pointed to an entry in the cheque register. The cheque was issued to C. Workman in the amount of forty dollars.

"There others like this. I can't find invoices to explain any of them. Moreover, I'm not aware of anyone named 'C. Workman' in the family. Albert's sons are named Evan and Henry, so it isn't them."

"Carlotta," I said.

She stared at the register and murmured, "Yes. I don't know what to do."

"We need to get as much information as possible before we act," I said.

We made a list of the dates and amounts of all cheques issued to C. Workman. The earliest date was the week after our final encounter with Carlotta.

"Have you looked in the canceled cheque box?" I asked.

She shook her head. "I was afraid to proceed alone. I believe I know what we'll find, and I'm not certain how to deal with it."

She retrieved the metal box in which processed cheques returned by the bank were filed. As we expected, every cheque issued to C. Workman was in Albert's handwriting. The markings on the back showed that all of them had been deposited to an account at People's Bank of Salinas, California, a small community about three hundred miles north.

I said, "The last time I saw Carlotta was in Albert's library. She had just confessed to the murder of Irene Clayton. She was in Albert's custody, and he said he intended to turn her over to Sheriff Jacobsen."

Laura frowned. "Martha Mae told me about the incident in detail, but I don't recall reading any newspaper reports of the matter. Is it possible that she was never arrested?"

Only then did I realize our oversight. The most probable reason that Carlotta's arrest had not been reported was that it did not occur. It would be a simple matter for her to live elsewhere unnoticed, provided that she had a reliable source of money.

"Don't reveal this to anyone just now," I said. "We need help."


I EXPECTED MANDY to be angry when she learned what Albert had done. Instead, she merely shrugged.

"For many people, certain loyalties take precedence over the law. Surely you must understand that," she said.

I felt a flash of anger. "But Carlotta killed Irene. She confessed to it in the presence of witnesses. Aren't you concerned about justice, for Irene's sake?"

"Of course I am. It was unrealistic of us to expect Albert to facilitate the arrest of his own daughter. We erred in not pursuing the matter ourselves."

I glared at her. "He's sent her a considerable sum of money. I suspect that he intends for her to continue to live quite comfortably."

"So it seems."

"So it seems?" My temper escalated. "*So it seems? We could have prevented this perfidy. Don't you think we ought to do something to remedy it?"

She was taken aback by my reaction. "Oh, sweetheart, once again I made the foolish assumption that your view of the matter was similar to mine." She put her hands on my shoulders. "I'll speak with Albert. We can't change the past, but perhaps we can convince him to alter the current arrangement." She shook her head. "I'm such a fool."

My heart melted. My kind, wonderful, brilliant, fearless lover was anything but a fool. How could I express all that I felt for her?

"I love you," I whispered.

She grinned. "We'll find a way through this. I promise."


WE MET LAURA at the Workman Ranch the following afternoon. Albert was sequestered in his office. The three of us entered and closed the door.

His smile disappeared when he saw our faces. "Is something wrong?"

Laura said, "As you know, I've been examining the business records for the past several days."

He nodded.

"I've found something irregular."

"Involving Peter Blaylock?"

"No, Albert. Involving you."

"Me? But what—"

Laura's tone was angry. "You've issued numerous cheques to Carlotta recently."

I said, "The first one was dated only days after the encounter in the library, when she confessed to killing Irene Clayton and attempted to kill Mandy."

He looked down at his desk and absently picked up a pencil. "I didn't think you would notice."

Mandy said, "I understand that your love for your daughter could make it difficult to play a role in her arrest."

"When I took Carlotta from the library that fateful night, I fully intended to deliver her to the sheriff. But I couldn't bring myself to do it. 'Difficult' is the incorrect word. It was, in fact, impossible."

"So you let her go," I said.

I recalled Carlotta's attempt to kill Mandy, and that she would have succeeded had Martha Mae not intervened. Albert was fully aware that his daughter was a ruthless killer. Although I understood the reason for his action, I could not bring myself to accept it.

He shrank into his chair. "What I did was dishonorable. I know that."

Laura said, "It was bad enough that you released Carlotta. It's worse that you've continued to enable her to evade justice."

"I don't know what I can do." He was on the verge of tears.

Mandy said, "Although she's your daughter, the fact remains that you have repeatedly aided and abetted a murderer. It's clear that this violates your own code of honor, so you'll have no peace of mind until you cease."

He nodded and murmured, "It will be difficult. But I will cease."

When I saw the agony reflected in his face, I knew for certain that Albert would keep his resolve. What I didn't realize at the time was the frightening and violent result his decision would bring.


WE PASSED AN uneventful month. The school term ended, so I was able to devote most of my time to improving our house and the little flower and vegetable gardens in the backyard. Although I continued to give a great deal of thought to the criminal activities that we had witnessed, everyone around me seemed to have forgotten them entirely.

Our lives returned abruptly to a state of chaos one afternoon when Laura arrived at our house. I responded to frantic pounding at the front door and found her in a state of near panic.

She trembled badly, choking back tears. "It's Carlotta. Carlotta has returned to the Workman Ranch."

"Are you certain?"

"Yes, although I might be the only person who is aware of it...aside from Albert."

"How can it be that nobody at the ranch saw her?" I asked.

"Several people did see her, but they didn't recognize her. She rode to the main house on an old mule. She was dressed as a widow in mourning, including a veil that covered her face."

Laura followed me to the kitchen, where I poured a glass of water for her. She drank half of it and continued.

"Her clothing was that of a much larger woman. I believe she must have strapped pillows or bundles of cloth to her body. She bent over a bit when she walked. She appeared to be old and fat."

"How did you discover her identity?"

"I was in one of the small offices, working on the ranch ledgers. I saw an old woman...what I believed at the time was an old woman...pass by in the hallway that leads to Albert's office. I thought nothing of it. A few minutes later, I came upon a transaction that I believed was entered incorrectly. The amount was significant, so I decided to ask Albert about it."

She paused while she finished her glass of water. "His office door was open. I could hear the voices of Albert and a woman, but I couldn't discern their conversation. The old woman's back was facing the office door. As I started to enter, she turned to the side and I saw her profile." Her voice began to shake. "It was Carlotta. I have absolutely no doubt."

"Did she see you?" I asked.

"No, but I'm not certain about Albert. I pulled back just as he began to look toward the door, where I was standing."

"You need to stay away from the ranch until Albert's intentions are clear," I said.

She nodded. "I fully intend to keep my distance."

THAT EVENING I related Laura's experience to Mandy. She looked at the floor and didn't speak for several minutes.

Finally she said, "I believe that Carlotta is here for two reasons. First, she wants money from Albert. Since she no longer receives his cheques by mail, she's come to apply pressure in person. Second, she wants revenge against me." She shrugged. "I still don't understand why she holds me accountable for her misfortune. Nevertheless, the fact remains that I am the target of her vengeance."

"Unfortunately, I'm afraid that you're entirely correct," I said.

Mandy said, "We can't be certain of Albert's reaction. But since he stopped sending cheques to Carlotta, I doubt that she trusts him to protect her." She stood and began to pace. "If I were Carlotta, I would secure whatever money I could from Albert, then exact revenge on my enemy at the last possible moment before leaving the area."

I said, "But we still don't know when —"

"The train!" She snapped her fingers. "She knows that I'm always in the Western Union Office at the railroad station whenever a passenger train is scheduled to stop. The northbound train will be here on Wednesday morning. It would be a brilliant maneuver to dispose of me just prior to boarding that train."

AS SHE PREPARED for her morning at the Western Union Office on Wednesday, Mandy was quieter than usual. Once again, she asked for my assurance that I would stay clear of the Chatsworth Park Railroad Station. I smiled and nodded. Ten minutes after her departure, I followed.

The station lobby was nearly empty when I entered. I could hear the muffled laughter of the men in the diner at the rear of the building. A man who appeared to be a ranch hand was engrossed in a magazine. Two nuns were engaged in whispered conversation. Martha Mae Kellogg, smiling demurely, sat across from the entry to the Western Union Office. I approached her immediately.

"What are you doing here?" I asked.

She said, "Please lower your voice, April. You know perfectly well what I'm doing here."

"Mandy said that she didn't tell anyone about...about what she expects will happen."

"That is correct. Mandy has no idea that I'm here. But Laura told me about her experience at the Workman Ranch. If you simply follow the facts to their logical conclusion, it's quite clear that Carlotta intends to kill Mandy and escape minutes afterward on the train." She looked at her watch. "I expect to see a fat old woman attired in black mourning garments at any moment."

"I believe she just arrived," I said.

The woman who entered the lobby matched Laura's description precisely. She walked slowly and methodically toward Mandy's office. When she entered, Martha Mae stood and walked to the doorway of the office.

I followed but stayed nearly out of sight for fear that my presence would have a negative impact. I saw the flash of recognition when Mandy set eyes first on the old woman and then an instant later on Martha Mae.

Mandy stepped to the counter. "How may I help you?" she asked.

"I want to know when the train will be here." She used a gravelly sound and an unidentifiable accent to disguise her voice.

Mandy said, "About five minutes. If you wish to send a wire, you need to hurry."

The woman reached into the folds of her voluminous robes and produced a Colt .45 pistol, which she pointed directly at Mandy.

"Five minutes is more than enough," she said. Carlotta's voice was no longer disguised.

"Perhaps while we wait you can explain why you blame me for all that's happened to you."

"That would require much more time than I have to spare," Carlotta said. "I should kill you based on the events of the past month alone — my father's sudden refusal to send the cheques I depend upon, and now his refusal to give me any money at all. He let it slip that you had a hand in those decisions."

As she pressed her derringer against Carlotta's neck, Martha Mae said, "You might want to reconsider what you're about to do. After all, if you pull that trigger, you won't live long enough to see the result. In fact, if you don't lower your gun immediately, you won't live long enough to see the next minute."

Carlotta put the gun on the counter, but her hand rested only a few inches from it. Neither Mandy nor Martha Mae appeared to notice.

Martha Mae turned her head slightly toward me. "April, the sheriff is back there in the diner. Would you be kind enough to summon him?"

As I turned to run, I collided with Albert so hard that I lost my balance and fell to the floor. In that instant, Martha Mae and Mandy took their eyes off Carlotta, and she seized her gun. In the next instant, Martha Mae fired her derringer and shattered Carlotta's wrist.

I scrambled on my hands and knees to secure the Colt .45 that had fallen to the floor a few feet away. I felt a sharp pain when Carlotta kicked me in the stomach. I didn't care. I had the gun. I struggled to my feet as Mandy and Martha Mae held her away from me.

"Papa, help me! These women...I've been shot!"

Albert shook his head. "Not this time, daughter. This time, we really will go to the sheriff." He looked at her wrist. "First we must visit

Dr. Halverson. Then, the sheriff."

"If you don't mind, Albert, I'll accompany the two of you," Martha Mae said sweetly.

He smiled. "Of course. I understand your concern."

She slipped the derringer into her handbag, winked at Mandy, and followed Albert and Carlotta out of the railroad station.

"Are you injured?" Mandy asked. "Carlotta kicked you hard."

I felt my stomach. "Most of the pain has subsided. I believe I'll be all right." I paused. "Do you trust Albert to deliver Carlotta to the sheriff?"

"Yes, I do. But even if I didn't, I wouldn't be concerned about the possibility of Carlotta's escape." She laughed. "After all, Martha Mae is on the case."

The train was an hour late. I stayed with Mandy at the railroad station until it departed and she closed the Western Union office.

When we went outside, I noticed a group of about a dozen people gathered at an open area along the railroad track a half mile north. From that distance, I couldn't see what had drawn them there. We turned south and went home. Only later did I learn what had occurred.

Local Woman Dies in Railroad Mishap
Special to the Times by M. T. Wells

Carlotta Workman, daughter of prominent San Fernando Valley rancher Albert Workman, died on Wednesday, August 20, when she was pulled under the wheels of a northbound passenger train. The mishap occurred about a half mile from the Chatsworth Park Railroad Station.

Witnesses reported that Miss Workman attempted to board the train while it was moving at approximately ten miles per hour, having left the station only minutes earlier.

According to sources close to the matter, Miss Workman was dressed in long robes which were caught beneath the wheels of a railroad car as she attempted to board it. Unable to extricate herself from her clothing, she was pulled under the moving train and died immediately. A private service was held on August 21 at Halverson Mortuary.

Mr. Joshua Cardell, representing the Southern Pacific Railroad Company, issued the following statement: "Southern Pacific deeply regrets the death of Miss Workman. The public is reminded once again that the only safe time to board a railroad car is when it is at a complete stop."

"WHAT DETAILS DID you withhold from your report?" I asked Mandy.

"Only a few. As you can see, I didn't report that Carlotta was taken to Doc Halverson's office for treatment of a gunshot wound. Nor did I bother to mention that his office is less than a block from the railroad track. Those details aren't germane to the story."

I smiled. "No, of course not. What I was asking about were the *germane* details."

"Oh. When they emerged from Doc Halverson's office, Carlotta was flanked by Albert and Martha Mae. They intended to deliver her directly to the sheriff. At that moment the train was approaching, still moving slowly. When it was less than twenty yards from where they stood, Carlotta broke away and ran toward it." She shrugged. "That's all."

"You haven't reported the details of Carlotta's crimes," I said.

"What purpose would it serve? In a roundabout way, she paid for Irene's murder with her life. As it stands, Albert is spared the family disgrace, so his honor is intact. I believe that the resolution is entirely satisfactory."

I said, "I agree."

# Chapter Twenty-one

I WAS GRATEFUL that the interminable series of unfortunate and stressful events appeared at last to have come to an end. We were settled into our permanent home, and my life began to feel normal.

The townspeople seemed to accept us. I read a recent novel by Henry James entitled *The Bostonians* which used the term "Boston marriage" to describe a cohabitant relationship between two unmarried women. The author did not explicitly address the issue of sex, but I found it difficult to imagine a Boston marriage that did not include a sexual relationship. Still, the possibility did exist, and apparently those around us who could not bring themselves to contemplate the reality of our situation chose to believe it. Unfortunately, there was an exception.

One afternoon while I was at home alone we had unexpected visitors. Hazel Moran and her husband Patrick appeared at the front door. As an upstairs maid at the Workman Ranch, Hazel was aware of our sleeping arrangements, and she had made no secret of her disapproval of us. In light of this, I was puzzled as to why the Morans had chosen to call on us. Nevertheless, I showed them to the parlor.

Without preamble, Hazel glared at me and said, "You two are unnatural."

"What is the purpose of your visit?" I asked her.

I didn't believe that they had come to our home merely to tell us that they did not approve of how we lived. I sensed a more sinister motive, and I wanted to know what it was before our conversation proceeded.

"If I tell certain people what I know, both of you will be outcasts. Nobody will speak to you. Nobody will do business with you." She leered at me triumphantly. "You won't be able to buy or sell anything in the entire San Fernando Valley."

I struggled to hide my anger. "Who are the 'certain people' and what would you tell them, Hazel?"

"People like all the merchants. People like the boss of the school where you teach. People like Albert Workman." Her exhilaration increased as she warmed to her task of threatening me. "I could tell all of them about the filthy things you women do in your bedroom."

"Do you plan to do this in the near future? Did you come here to warn me about it?"

By way of a reply, I expected their demand for a specific amount of money. I was not disappointed.

Patrick spoke for the first time. "This unpleasantness can be avoided. Knowing what you women are doing is painful to us, but you could alleviate our distress. As long as you give us five dollars every month, we can keep our torment to ourselves."

That, apparently, was the full extent of their scheme. For five dollars per month, until they decided to increase the amount, the Morans would refrain from revealing our relationship.

I stood and said, "Mandy isn't here at the moment. But I'll explain the situation to her this evening."

"We'll return tomorrow afternoon at three o'clock. We expect your response at that time," Hazel said as we walked to the door. "Otherwise...." She fell silent, leaving me to imagine what horrors they intended to inflict upon us.

BY THE TIME she arrived home, Mandy had already learned of the Morans' scheme. They had paid a call on Laura and Martha Mae earlier in the day and made similar threats, which Martha Mae promptly relayed to Mandy.

"What can we do?" I asked.

She said, "Look at the facts. Hazel Moran has nothing more than a tale of which beds at the Workman Ranch were slept in or not slept in, and perhaps some vague idea of what it might mean. We haven't broken any laws...at least not since we left Palm Springs."

"No, but—"

"However, there are laws against extortion and attempted extortion."

I said, "But we have no proof of their scheme. If we were to report it, they could merely deny it and cause us to appear foolish and paranoid."

"True. But if there were eyewitnesses, they couldn't possibly deny it. Martha Mae and I analyzed the situation in depth. There is an element of risk, but we have a strategy that might resolve the matter to our satisfaction."

She explained the plan. The risk she referred to was associated with trusting both Carl Jacobsen and Albert Workman to support our position. Because neither man had ever mentioned the nature of our relationship, we had no idea if they were aware of it, or whether they could accept or even tolerate it. Nevertheless, we could think of no other satisfactory way to resolve the problem. Mandy said that she would ask Carl and Albert for their assistance.

THE FOLLOWING AFTERNOON at around two-thirty, both men arrived at our house. Mandy put their horses and Albert's wagon inside the barn and closed the doors. I made a pot of coffee. The four of us sat at the kitchen table and waited.

The Morans arrived shortly after three o'clock. Mandy answered the door and brought them to the parlor, where I was seated.

"I assume April explained everything," Patrick Moran said.

Mandy said, "The way she tells it, it's all a bit of a jumble. I'm not certain that I understand what you want."

Hazel said, "It's quite simple, you disgusting pervert. Either you give us five dollars every month or we tell everyone for miles around that you're a sexual deviant."

Mandy turned back to Patrick. "Is that correct, Mr. Moran?"

"That sums it up," he said. "You have a choice. Either pay us, or we start talking."

"Have you heard enough?" Mandy asked.

The Morans looked at each other. The question made no sense to them.

"Yes, we have," came a reply from just outside the parlor. Sheriff Carl Jacobsen and Albert Workman entered. "We have laws regarding extortion," Carl said.

Incredibly, the Morans took the position that their action was justified due to the nature of our "crime." They were unconcerned that the sheriff had overheard their threats.

Patrick said, "We've done nothing wrong, Sheriff. But these women have committed crimes against nature. They deserve whatever they get."

"They're nothing more than disgusting perverts," Hazel said.

Albert said, "Nothing more? These ladies were guests in my home. As my employee, I entrusted you with taking care of their needs. Instead, you violated my trust and made slanderous accusations against them."

"The accusations are true," she said.

He shook his head. "You don't understand, Hazel. Whether your accusations are true or false is irrelevant. What matters is that you made them, and in so doing you violated my trust. Effective immediately, you are no longer employed by the Workman Ranch."

Patrick stepped over to Carl and said, "Sheriff, because of these warped women, my wife is unemployed. As one man to another, I insist that you do something."

"I certainly can do something," Carl said. "I can arrest you and your wife for attempted extortion, which I personally witnessed." He shrugged. "Unless the ladies have another solution."

Mandy said, "Conviction of attempted extortion carries a prison sentence. If the Morans were to be arrested, they surely would be convicted, in light of the fact that the sheriff was an eyewitness to their crime. But we would gain nothing."

"Do you have an alternative suggestion?" Carl asked.

She nodded. "As long as the Morans refrain from speaking or writing about us, as well as Martha Mae Kellogg and Laura Workman, I see no need to pursue this any further. If, however, they choose to speak out on the matter, then I believe that it will become necessary to make the arrests."

"That's blackmail," Hazel shrieked. "You're blackmailing us!"

Carl said, "On the contrary, Mrs. Moran. You and your husband attempted to inflict serious harm on these ladies, with no justification whatsoever. As long as you refrain from besmirching their reputations, you will remain free despite your crime. I believe that their offer is quite generous. You may leave now."

It was clear that the Morans had not fully absorbed what had happened. Mandy saw them to the door, then returned to the parlor.

Albert said, "I must apologize for Hazel's despicable behavior. I had no idea that her character was flawed to that degree."

"And we in turn owe you a debt of gratitude," Mandy said. "You can depend on our loyalty in the future."

Carl said, "I don't believe that the Morans will cause you more grief." He grinned. "We can't afford to lose a good schoolteacher and the only decent telegraph operator in Chatsworth Park."

I said, "We appreciate your assistance, Carl. You know, unmarried women living as—"

"Stop!" he said. "I don't know anything about your personal lives. Please don't reveal any secrets to me."

After a final round of thanks and congratulations, Carl and Albert left. We burst into laughter and hugged each other tightly. Then we remembered that Laura and Martha Mae were awaiting the results of our meeting.

We hitched Daisy to the wagon and set out for their house to share the good news. As we rode, I pondered our circumstances.

"Do you suppose they know about us?" I asked.

She smiled. "They know it's possible that we're lovers. But as long as nobody confirms it, they can ignore the question. And as long as they can ignore the question, they'll be happy to count us among their friends and neighbors."

I said, "I agree. Do you think we might be able to move forward without further macabre experiences?"

After a moment's reflection, she said, "Quite possibly. Times are changing rapidly. I don't believe that the methods we've always used to resolve our problems will be appropriate in the future. I expect that our lives will be more ordered. And better."

# Epilogue

AS USUAL, MANDY was correct. We were happy, after so much turmoil, to achieve a life of tranquility. The San Fernando Valley began to take on the trappings of modern civilization. Technology was changing our lives at an incredible rate and in unforeseen ways.

The World's Columbian Exhibition in Chicago was open to the public from May through October. Scientists and historians declared that 1893 was a pivotal year in modern history. There were numerous reports from the "Chicago World's Fair," as it came to be called, of functioning inventions that were considered mere flights of fancy just ten years earlier. Thomas Edison, George Westinghouse and Nikola Tesla became household names.

We pondered how electricity might help to resolve the water situation. Because agriculture was the predominant industry, annual economic success or failure was linked inextricably to water, the most prized asset of the San Fernando Valley. There had been consecutive years of flooding, during which crops were ruined. More often, there had been consecutive years of drought, during which all crops and most livestock were lost. There had been high-stakes battles regarding who owned the precious water that flowed through rivers, creeks, and over countless privately owned parcels of land.

Since electricity could power machinery, it seemed logical that it could somehow be used to pump, move, drain, and store water. There was speculation that electricity could enhance the existing capability of transferring water from the northern mountains via aqueduct. But the solution remained out of reach.

As the central section of Los Angeles continued to expand, more people moved to the outlying areas. Landowners began to subdivide some of their property into parcels suitable in size for small farms or ranches. Commercial enterprises sprang up to meet the needs of the constant influx of people.

A real estate speculator offered to purchase five hundred acres of Laura's land in Chatsworth Park for the astonishing sum of two thousand dollars. Having no need for money, she rejected the proposal. But the incident served to open our eyes to the extent of the transition occurring around us.

The era of frontier life is coming to an end. Mandy has speculated that the population of the Los Angeles area might someday exceed that of San Francisco. Although I have grown accustomed to her uncanny powers of perception, I am unable to believe that she is correct in this instance. Nevertheless, it is clear to me that the future will be radically different from the present. Hopefully, women like us — Mandy, Laura,

Martha Mae and me — will have an easier life.

Without any biological descendants, it is doubtful that our lives will be recorded or remembered. But if by chance the knowledge of our existence survives, my hope is that one fact should be known: we did the best we could.

April Reynolds
Chatsworth Park, California
December 16, 1893

# Author's Note

When I read historical fiction, I often wonder how much of it is based on fact. My characters are a product of my imagination, but many of the events in their lives really happened. Here's an overview of actual history.

The Sonoran earthquake, with an estimated magnitude of 7.4, really did occur in Arizona in 1877. While the earthquake's impact on the Lost Dutchman Mine is speculation, the fortune has never been found, and the legend of the mine still lives.

The Southern Pacific Railroad completed the route through Palm Springs in 1877, which enabled early settlers to establish the area as a popular tourist destination. The Palm Springs Hotel was built in 1886, and was an immediate success.

In the San Fernando Valley, the prosperous Workman Ranch consisted of thirteen thousand acres. Today, all that remains of the ranch is the main house, which is maintained by the City of Los Angeles within Shadow Ranch Park. The Chatsworth Park Railroad Station was opened in 1893, and was destroyed by fire in 1917. That area today is the site of the Metrolink and Amtrak stations in Chatsworth.

# Other Vicki Stevenson Titles:

## *Family Values*

Devastated by the collapse of her long-term relationship, Alice Cruz decides to begin life anew. She moves to a small town, rents an apartment, and establishes a career in real estate. But when she tries to liquidate some of her investments for a down payment on a house, she discovers that she has been victimized by a con artist.

Local resident Tyler Sorensen has a track record of countless affairs without any emotional involvement. Known for her sexy good looks, easygoing kindness, and unique approach to problems, Tyler is asked by a mutual friend to figure out how Alice can recover her money.

While Tyler's elaborate plan progresses and members of her LGBT family work toward the solution, they discover that the con game involves more people and far higher stakes than they had imagined. As the family encounters unexpected obstacles, Tyler and Alice struggle with a growing emotional connection deeper than either woman has ever experienced.

ISBN: 978-1-932300-89-5
eBook ISBN: 978-1-935053-67-5

## *Family Affairs*

Assigned to work undercover in a small-town nursing home, insurance investigator Stacey Gardner sets out to find fraudulent medical claims. When she meets local resident Liz Schroeder, romance begins to bloom. But then she discovers widespread elder abuse of which the entire nursing home staff is aware, and she fears that the whole town may be participating in a cover-up.

Liz persuades Stacey to trust her and to accept help from her LGBT family in exposing the abuse. The family discovers an elaborate scheme that seems to defy exposure. Many of the nursing home staff members are dedicated to stopping Stacey at any cost, and the rest are too intimidated to reveal any information.

The family presses on, determined to bring justice to the perpetrators and relief to the suffering patients. While the bond of love between Stacey and Liz grows ever stronger, they face the agonizing reality that success will mean a new assignment for Stacey, and her subsequent departure will spell the end of the chance at happiness that both women desperately crave.

ISBN: 978-1-932300-97-0
eBook ISBN: 978-1-935053-69-9

## *Family Ties*

Fleeing from her abusive husband, Jill Dewey impulsively returns to her small hometown. A chance encounter with a former teacher leads her to the safety of a local dude ranch, where she accepts work as a chef. Through an intermediary, she notifies her parents that she is well and does not wish to be found.

Ranch owner Casey McQuaid is pleased with Jill's performance as a chef and enjoys her company as a friend. Jill is drawn to the warmth and support of Casey's LGBT family. As she becomes involved in the family's struggle against a powerful adversary of the gay community, she is increasingly obsessed by unexpected feelings for Casey.

While Jill grapples with her newly emerging emotions, her parents and husband discover her whereabouts and work relentlessly and viciously to compel her to return. And as the battle against the homophobic enemy proceeds, Casey and Jill must confront the nature of the relationship that has developed between them.

ISBN: 978-1-935053-03-3
eBook ISBN: 978-1-935053-67-5

## *Certain Personal Matters*

The unexpected death of her brother Tony brings Amy Dalton to an Arizona tourist town where she meets Dusty Hardin, owner of a jeep rental agency. Even under the dark cloud of Tony's death, the chemistry between Dusty and Amy is undeniable and unstoppable, and their relationship begins to flourish.

When it becomes clear that her brother died under suspicious circumstances, Amy sets out to discover the facts. Her inquiries uncover a link to a crime that took place years ago, awakening a long dormant town scandal. Dusty and her LGBT family join Amy in her pursuit of justice, but cunning and powerful influences are at work to deny their success. As the relationship between Amy and Dusty reaches sizzling heights, so does the danger to everyone involved while they strive to find and expose the maniacal force determined to suppress the truth.

ISBN: 978-1-935053-06-4
eBook ISBN: 978-1-935053-70-5

# Callie's Dilemma

While attending a convention for authors and fans of chick lit, Callie Delaney, closeted reigning queen of mainstream romance, meets Dale Kirby, irresistible fitness instructor for the health club at the hotel that's hosting the event. She also inadvertently walks into the prelude to a murder. Although Callie is unaware of the significance of what she sees, the killer is not, and he embarks on a relentless campaign to eliminate the only witness to his crime.

With help from Dale's LGBT family, the women set out to uncover the motivation for the threats against Callie, identify her mysterious stalker, and ultimately prove him guilty of murder. As a fragile relationship develops between Dale and Callie, they are forced to confront escalating danger and the irresolvable conflict between the demands of Callie's public image and the reality of her personal desire.

ISBN: 978-1-61929-003-7
eBook ISBN: 978-1-61929-004-4

# Other Yellow Rose books you may enjoy:

## Heart's Resolve
### by Carrie Carr

Gibson Proctor, a Park Police Officer for the Texas Department of Parks & Wildlife, has returned after twenty years to the rural area she once called home. She's able to easily adapt to the slower pace of the farming communities that surround the town of Benton, Texas, and tries her best to handle the expectations of her family, as well. Gib's comfortable existence is set into a tailspin when she unwittingly offends Delaney Kavanagh, the fiery-tempered architect who's in charge of repairing the spillway at Lake Kichai.

Although Delaney is currently in a relationship, she can't seem to get the amiable officer out of her mind. Not used to the type of attention she receives from the chivalrous woman, Delaney keeps waiting for the "real" Gib to show up. Will she ever accept Gib's acts of kindness as truth, or will she be content to stay in a relationship where she has to fight for everything?

ISBN 978-1-61929-051-8
eBook ISBN 978-1-61929-05

## Jess
### by Pauline George

Jess is a modern day lesbian Lothario who was so hurt from an emotionally damaging relationship that now she doesn't let anyone get close. She protects herself by keeping her relationships short and sweet. When Jess's sister Josie challenges her to get to know a woman before she jumps into bed with her, Jess is intrigued. How hard can that be?

Although she's a serial monogamist, Jess has deep-seated morals that will be tested to the limit by her carefree acceptance of Josie's challenge. When she falls for her sister's best friend Katie, she suddenly finds her life upended, and she's left wondering if she actually has what it takes to have a lasting and fulfilling relationship. Is she destined to spend her life bed-hopping? Will her ever-growing attraction to Katie be the catalyst for romance, or will Katie's indecision about her life prove to be Jess's downfall?

ISBN 978-1-61929-138-6
eBook ISBN 978-1-61929-139-3

# The Gardner of Aria Manor
## by A.L. Duncan

Janie O'Grady is a woman quite adapted to her life and circumstances as they are, living in New York City during the Great Depression. A hint of cynicism clouds the cold winter streets and keeps the rum runners strange bedfellows to the Irish mob's bounty in and out of speakeasy's, daring to brush shoulders with the neighboring Italian mobs. At a moment where Janie fears for her life she is presented with circumstances which seem like a harsh nudge from the heavens to decide her own destiny.

Feeling there is no other choice, Janie makes the fateful decision to change her identity and move to the Devon countryside on the coastal shores of England, as a Head Gardener to a 17th century manor, where déjà vu and the intrigues of a past life and murder mystery overshadow her life in the big city.

This tale invites you to peek into the pages of one woman's life and follow her incredible story of self-discovery of a very different kind; where looking back at one's past includes connecting the threads of passions and desires of a life lived before. A life lived where one's odyssey must wait to complete the circle in the next life.

ISBN: 978-1-61929-158-4
eBook ISBN 978-1-61929-1-159-1

# Second Chances
## by Lynne Norris

Alex Margulies is a self-driven chief attending physician in the emergency department of a large community medical center. She is fierce and merciless with her staff, expecting the same tireless dedication from her peers as she does from herself.

Driven by her recent failures, Alex struggles to put her troubled past behind her. With the annual influx of new residents to the hospital, she meets one of her new charges, Regina Kingston, a bright, young, promising doctor. Before long, Regina finds herself irresistibly drawn to the enigmatic physician despite the woman's fiery personality and maligned reputation.

As professional differences come to light and personalities clash, Alex and Regina both struggle to overcome their own demons. It is within each other that they will find the strength to overcome their darkest moments, surviving to live and love again.

**This is an Author's Cut Edition released in eBook formats only**

eBook ISBN 978-1-61929-172-0

# OTHER YELLOW ROSE PUBLICATIONS

| | | |
|---|---|---|
| Brenda Adcock | Soiled Dove | 978-1-935053-35-4 |
| Brenda Adcock | The Sea Hawk | 978-1-935053-10-1 |
| Brenda Adcock | The Other Mrs. Champion | 978-1-935053-46-0 |
| Brenda Adcock | Picking Up the Pieces | 978-1-61929-120-1 |
| Brenda Adcock | The Game of Denial | 978-1-61929-130-0 |
| Janet Albert | Twenty-four Days | 978-1-935053-16-3 |
| Janet Albert | A Table for Two | 978-1-935053-27-9 |
| Janet Albert | Casa Parisi | 978-1-61929-015-0 |
| Georgia Beers | Thy Neighbor's Wife | 1-932300-15-5 |
| Georgia Beers | Turning the Page | 978-1-932300-71-0 |
| Carrie Brennan | Curve | 978-1-932300-41-3 |
| Carrie Carr | Destiny's Bridge | 1-932300-11-2 |
| Carrie Carr | Faith's Crossing | 1-932300-12-0 |
| Carrie Carr | Hope's Path | 1-932300-40-6 |
| Carrie Carr | Love's Journey | 978-1-932300-65-9 |
| Carrie Carr | Strength of the Heart | 978-1-932300-81-9 |
| Carrie Carr | The Way Things Should Be | 978-1-932300-39-0 |
| Carrie Carr | To Hold Forever | 978-1-932300-21-5 |
| Carrie Carr | Trust Our Tomorrows | 978-1-61929-011-2 |
| Carrie Carr | Piperton | 978-1-935053-20-0 |
| Carrie Carr | Something to Be Thankful For | 1-932300-04-X |
| Carrie Carr | Diving Into the Turn | 978-1-932300-54-3 |
| Carrie Carr | Heart's Resolve | 978-1-61929-051-8 |
| J M Carr | Hard Lessons | 978-1-61929-162-1 |
| Sharon G. Clark | A Majestic Affair | 978-1-61929-178-2 |
| Sky Croft | Amazonia | 978-1-61929-066-2 |
| Sky Croft | Amazonia: An Impossible Choice | 978-1-61929-180-5 |
| Sky Croft | Mountain Rescue: The Ascent | 978-1-61929-098-3 |
| Cronin and Foster | Blue Collar Lesbian Erotica | 978-1-935053-01-9 |
| Cronin and Foster | Women in Uniform | 978-1-935053-31-6 |
| Pat Cronin | Souls' Rescue | 978-1-935053-30-9 |
| Verda Foster | The Gift | 978-1-61929-029-7 |
| Verda Foster | The Chosen | 978-1-61929-027-3 |
| Verda Foster | These Dreams | 978-1-61929-025-9 |
| Anna Furtado | The Heart's Desire | 1-932300-32-5 |
| Anna Furtado | The Heart's Strength | 978-1-932300-93-2 |
| Anna Furtado | The Heart's Longing | 978-1-935053-26-2 |
| Melissa Good | Eye of the Storm | 1-932300-13-9 |
| Melissa Good | Hurricane Watch | 978-1-935053-00-2 |
| Melissa Good | Moving Target | 978-1-61929-150-8 |
| Melissa Good | Red Sky At Morning | 978-1-932300-80-2 |
| Melissa Good | Storm Surge: Book One | 978-1-935053-28-6 |
| Melissa Good | Storm Surge: Book Two | 978-1-935053-39-2 |
| Melissa Good | Stormy Waters | 978-1-61929-082-2 |
| Melissa Good | Thicker Than Water | 1-932300-24-4 |
| Melissa Good | Terrors of the High Seas | 1-932300-45-7 |
| Melissa Good | Tropical Storm | 978-1-932300-60-4 |
| Melissa Good | Tropical Convergence | 978-1-935053-18-7 |
| Regina A. Hanel | Love Another Day | 978-1-935053-44-6 |
| Jeanine Hoffman | Lights & Sirens | 978-1-61929-114-0 |

## About the Author

Vicki Stevenson toiled for years as a computer programmer, systems analyst, and eventually Manager of Office Automation for a large defense contractor. Finally striking out on her own, she became a consultant to a computer component manufacturer, where she worked as a designer, writer, and trainer of manufacturing automation for semiconductors. She has a BA in Economics from UCLA.

In addition to writing fiction, Vicki's hobbies are daydreaming, snacking, and procrastination. She lives with her partner Sara, the love of her life. After an engagement of twenty-one years, fifteen of them in Arizona, they moved home to California and got married. How sweet it is.

# VISIT US ONLINE AT
www.regalcrest.biz

## At the Regal Crest Website You'll Find

- The latest news about forthcoming titles and new releases

- Our complete backlist of romance, mystery, thriller and adventure titles

- Information about your favorite authors

- Current bestsellers

- Media tearsheets to print and take with you when you shop

- Which books are also available as eBooks.


Regal Crest print titles are available from all progressive booksellers including numerous sources online. Our distributors are Bella Distribution and Ingram.